LP LONG

Long, Elliot
Wassala Valley Shootout.

ATCHISON PUBLIC LIBRARY
401 Kansas
Atchison, KS 66002

ATCHISON LIBRARY
401 KANSAS
ATCHISON, KS 66002

SPECIAL MESSAGE TO READERS

This book is published by
THE ULVERSCROFT FOUNDATION
a registered charity in the U.K., No. 264873

The Foundation was established in 1974 to provide funds to help towards research, diagnosis and treatment of eye diseases. Below are a few examples of contributions made by THE ULVERSCROFT FOUNDATION:

A new Children's Assessment Unit at Moorfield's Hospital, London.

•

Twin operating theatres at the Western Ophthalmic Hospital, London.

•

The Frederick Thorpe Ulverscroft Chair of Ophthalmology at the University of Leicester.

•

Eye Laser equipment to various eye hospitals.

If you would like to help further the work of the Foundation by making a donation or leaving a legacy, every contribution, no matter how small, is received with gratitude. Please write for details to:

**THE ULVERSCROFT FOUNDATION,
The Green, Bradgate Road, Anstey,
Leicester LE7 7FU. England
Telephone: (0533)364325**

WASSALA VALLEY SHOOTOUT

Hannibal Mosely rested his hand on the holstered Colt at his hip and demanded to know if Maddon had killed his boy. Frank Maddon met the rancher's piercing stare and told him he was sorry but he had had no choice as the boy pulled a gun on him. He watched Mosely's cold stare narrow and moved his hand close to the gun on his left hip. The rancher stated boldly that he was going to kill him. It was Frank Maddon's first day in Wassala Valley, and he had no intention of allowing it to be his last . . .

ELLIOT LONG

WASSALA VALLEY SHOOTOUT

Complete and Unabridged

First published in Great Britain in 1991 by
Robert Hale Limited, London

First Linford Edition
published November 1993
by arrangement with
Robert Hale Limited, London

The right of Elliot Long to be identified as
the author of this work has been asserted by
him in accordance with the
Copyright, Designs and Patents Act, 1988

Copyright © 1991 by Elliot Long
All rights reserved

British Library CIP Data

Long, Elliot
 Wassala Valley shootout.—Large print ed.—
 Linford western library
 I. Title II. Series
 813.54 [F]

ISBN 0-7089-7444-9

Published by
F. A. Thorpe (Publishing) Ltd.
Anstey, Leicestershire

Set by Words & Graphics Ltd.
Anstey, Leicestershire
Printed and bound in Great Britain by
T. J. Press (Padstow) Ltd., Padstow, Cornwall

This book is printed on acid-free paper

To:
Elizabeth, Richard and Susan,
my dear children.

1

THE rider had been head-down following him through the hills for five hours now and Frank Maddon had had enough of it. First off, there was no damned reason for it as far as he knew. And second — it gave him an icy, prickly feeling down his backbone he could well do without.

He narrowed his brown, serious eyes, his face grim, and he urged his bay up the trail through the gap in the yellow rocks that tumbled haphazardly down the hillside.

Fifty yards or so on, he turned the bay into hiding deep in the spruce clustered there, dismounted and tethered it. Then he back-tracked to the gap and waited, the noon sun burning his back through his waistcoat and grey cotton shirt.

Hearing the approaching scrape of hooves on rock ten minutes later, he tightened up, his senses heightening. His man was almost to the gap before Maddon stepped out, his business-like, short-barrelled Peacemaker firm in his left hand and levelled at the man's navel.

"Right," he demanded evenly. "Hold it. Jest what the hell — "

To Maddon's amazement the crazy galoot's hand streaked for gun-metal, a vicious snarl distorting his face.

"You're goin' to get what's coming to you, Maddon!" he shouted.

Lead was burning a path across Maddon's cheek before he let off his own piece, his astonishment was so complete. He'd never seen this hombre before in his life!

Maddon watched the man pile back off his superb palomino, heard the man's second shot rattling harmlessly through the trees behind him.

Now the man dropped heavily to the rocky trail floor and Maddon saw bright blood immediately blossom on his fancy silk shirt front, staining the buckskin jacket over it.

And Maddon knew the man's heart had been shattered by his bullet. He had made it his policy to rarely need a second shot to finish an argument at this range. That was why he was still alive and forty-four years of age.

Now slow anger replaced Maddon's astonishment. What, in the name of God, did the crazy bastard hope to gain by doing that? And how did he come to know his name?

Maddon looked into the man's grey eyes. They were staring sightlessly past him — straight into the brassy sun directly above them. And already the glaze of death was developing in them.

Then Maddon watched the crimson streak of blood, running across the man's cheek from his agape mouth, come to a halt near his left ear. It almost seemed to Maddon the damned fool was grinning at him.

Disgusted by such an unnecessary

waste of life, Maddon slowly placed his smoking Colt Peacemaker back into its well-oiled, well-used holster, his nose stinging with the acrid stench of the gunsmoke floating about him in the calm air.

The sound of their guns still crashed around in the mountains behind him. Damn it, Maddon thought fretfully now, it was the last thing he wanted — noise. He knew these hills were lousy with bronco Apaches.

He dabbed the lead-burn on his cheek with his bandana and studied the man's fancy, but blood-stained, clothes. He wore a superior buckskin jacket and a frilly blue silk shirt. Also, he wore finely tooled boots into which were tucked grey trousers of good quality.

Maddon lifted his gaze to the silver-studded saddle on the back of the man's palomino stallion, which was now stood cropping the sparse grass nearby. That saddle had sure cost a hell of a lot more than thirty dollars, too, Maddon studied. Even the gun-rig around the man's waist was tooled with fine scrolling, and a small silver copy of a vicious Mexican spur-rowel decorated the outside of the holster.

Maddon shook his head grimly. Damn it. All he had wanted was for the man to answer the question why he was trailing him, peaceful-like. Now he was a dead man and it galled Maddon to be the man that had had to do it. Not because of any aversion to dealing death if the circumstances called for it. This had been unnecessary.

Slowly he scrubbed his dark, three-day-old beard with a long-fingered, sinewy hand, his calm brown eyes still surveying the man's admittedly handsome features. He must have some identification about him, Maddon decided now.

Still irritated that he had been placed in this position, he bent and searched through the man's clothing. Finally he came up with a letter. It was addressed to Hannibal Mosely, Rowel Ranch, c/o

General Stores, Clayton, Territory of New Mexico. Inside was information about what price beef on the hoof was making at the Wichita sales.

He'd heard of the Rowel. By all the accounts it was one of the largest spreads hereabouts. And he knew it bordered on his brother Holly's place. And judging by the dude clothes and silver-studded saddle, the dead man was no twenty dollar cowpoke. But on further consideration he looked too young to be owner. He could be no more than maybe twenty-five years of age at the most.

Son? Maddon wondered speculatively.

Slowly he rose from his crouched position and stared disgruntled into the distance, ignoring the sun scalding his back. Once again he pulled out his brother's telegraph, the thing that had brought him here and read the communication thoughtfully:

FRANK I NEED YOU. EXPLAIN WHEN YOU ARRIVE.
HOLLY.

Always he and Holly had kept in touch. Maddon figured, because they were identical twins, they were somehow bonded together spiritually, thus putting their feelings for each other over and above just being ordinary kinfolk.

When Martha, his wife ...

Maddon's hard eyes softened for a moment at the thought of her. Then his heart skipped a beat — the pain, which always came with the memory of the manner of her death, numbing him. He licked his lips, his bleak eyes narrowing.

... When his wife, Martha, had been shot down by that crazy, whisky-soaked cowpoke during a hurrah-ing at Cedar Creek — a lesser-known trail town in which he had had his general store business — his peaceful way of life had been destroyed for ever.

Within an hour of Martha dying in his arms he had sought out Marshal Flute Maser and signed on as the deputy marshal Flute had so badly needed. Six blood-soaked months later

Maddon had left the now peaceful town with the reputation of being a mean man with a gun. He had become a saddle-tramp, the roots Martha had given him gone.

Now he was a feared bounty hunter. And he didn't give a damn about the taint the profession had either. He gave his quarry a lawman's deal. If he didn't like it . . . so be it.

Though he wandered freely, always he would make the nearest big town in the area he was operating his base, and he always let Holly know where he could find him. So when the telegraph reached him he had packed his possibles and raised dust, heading for the Wassala Valley where he knew Holly had his spread.

From this high vantage point in the dry, yellow hills he was travelling through, he looked with hard eyes beyond the rocky, undulating land he was in, to the green land spreading away towards the ranks of blue mountains in the far distance.

That green land in-between — Wassala Valley — was better land than he was in at the moment. He looked about him. This was a dry, desolate land, lumped west of blue, distant, white-tipped peaks. But even so, it was a beautiful land. And, he instinctively knew, a deadly land.

A man could die alone here and no one would ever know. The vast wastes would swallow him up like an owl swallows a mouse. Pretty soon his flesh would be grains of dust, his bones bleached — probably to lie undiscovered for a thousand years . . .

Maddon thought bleakly, he could roll this man into the brush, leave him there and that would be the end of it. He had a more than unpleasant feeling lurking within him that if he took this hombre into Clayton, the big town in Wassala Valley, he would be in deep trouble.

He killed the thought stone dead. Leave the man for coyote meat? The squalid idea disgusted him. And, damn it, he had nothing to hide. The crazy devil had pulled on him, and had got what he asked for. And, thinking again, Maddon knew if he left the man to such a fate he would have him on his conscience for the rest of his life, anyway.

What effect the shooting would have in Clayton was a bridge he would have to cross when he came to it. He fingered the oft-used sixgun pouched in an easily accessible position on his left hip, his eyes narrow. What worried him more was the fact that the shootout maybe wouldn't help Holly, being a neighbour of the Rowel spread. He was beginning to have a strong suspicion this man could be kin to the folks who owned the Rowel, judging by the trappings he wore and the saddle over the palomino.

The chitter of a bird on the still, savagely hot noon air caused him to tense. His conjectures died. His raw-boned frame froze. He ignored the sweat dripping off his forehead — didn't feel other sweat rolling down his back and thighs under his salt-patched shirt and worn levis.

He'd never heard that particular feathered friend do his warbling this time of day before — never.

He hunkered into a low crouch, his Colt already out and gripped in his left fist. He silently cursed the corpse lying dead at his feet.

Off left, the stranger's palomino began to stir restlessly now, its ears twitching. Maddon licked his suddenly dry lips. He knew he had to move from this position and quick.

He made for the cover of the brush immediately, his hard body bent low to the ground. He moved swiftly, but silently. He cursed the fact that he had left his horse tethered back in the trees.

Now Maddon felt the full, scalding force of the sun on his back as he padded forward. He'd have to work his way into the best position he could find. He blinked sweat out of his eyes.

Then take what the day offered from there . . .

And, as usual, he found his senses sharpening, keening up onto that other plane they rose to in situations like this — so that every sound, no matter how small, every change in the mood and sensations of the big land around him meant something.

And it was the brush of soft moccasin leather on hard grit seconds later, barely audible behind him that put him into a blurring turn, his gun coming up. His shot took the almost naked, breech-clouted Apache as he came boring down on him, his big knife poised to strike death.

The bronco whooped despairingly as he realised he was a dying man, that his life-blood was spurting out of the hole in his stomach, but still he came on.

This time, because of the buck's momentary faltering, Maddon was more deliberate. His next hunk of lead battered a bloody path through the bronco's brain causing him to collapse and sprawl, twitching spasmodically, at Maddon's feet.

The redskin's anguished knife-strike rasped into the soil inches from Maddon's left, dust-yellowed boot.

Maddon didn't pause to examine the bronco. He knew he had to move; knew the cry that had escaped the brave was more than one of pain. It was a warning call as well. Maddon reckoned there had to be at least one buck — or even more — at this moment homing in on the noise their meeting and his gun had created.

But with a quick intuitive thought, he gave vent to the chittering cry of the Apache's bird-call with practised ease, then he slithered carefully and quickly away from the spot, creeping around the thorn bushes and rocky outcrops, shallowing his breathing to pick up any little sound that came his way.

After moments the nervous little bird call came in return, shivering plaintive notes on the burning air, and satisfaction settled in Maddon.

Like a hawk seeing prey, he turned brown, hard eyes towards the spot.

And he felt comforted. The Indian wasn't sure what the situation was, Maddon assumed now, with reasonable confidence. He returned the call and moved another thirty yards south and waited.

The bronco popped up cautiously, two minutes later, sighting over an eroding yellow boulder above and to the right of Maddon. The brave's gaze was immediately drawn towards the palomino, now unconcernedly cropping grass again. The Apache's red headband showed starkly against his raven hair. And his brown right hand rested on top of the boulder, clasping an old Sharps carbine.

Satisfied his ruse had worked, Maddon laid the barrel of his Peacemaker across his right forearm and steadied it, sighting down the blue-grey barrel plumb centre of the red headband. It was a long shot for his short-barrelled handgun. But he felt confident and he pressured the trigger evenly.

The roar of the Colt was again intruding on the timeless silence of the hills. Through the acrid gunsmoke, Maddon watched the Apache's mouth disappear, blood spurting out, then his bullet tear on, ripping away the bronco's left cheekbone and ear as it exited.

Maddon watched the Apache, now maddened with pain, rear up, suddenly unmindful of his safety and sighting the Sharps down on Maddon.

Maddon rolled, scrambling to make himself a moving target, desperately knowing he was right under the bronco's gun.

The Sharps whacked hard sound into the hills. Maddon felt the Apache's lead stinging its way across his back, causing him to cry out. But it didn't stop him pausing and lining up again on the bronco. He knew it was a single-shot weapon the bronco had and he had used up most of his chances.

The brave was turning now, diving

for cover, his ruined face gushing blood. Maddon released his second shot. With satisfaction, he heard the dull, rasping cry of pain from the Apache as he disappeared below the yellow, dome-headed rock.

Grim-faced now, Maddon scanned the country around him for signs of other activity. Looked as though there was only the two of them, he ascertained with cautious relief. But he also knew that the one up there was still in the fight. And it took no imagination to know a wounded Apache was a dangerous Apache.

He grimaced as sweat-salt caused stinging pain to come to the graze in his back and he felt slow blood seeping down the groove between the big muscles lining his backbone.

He knew the wound wasn't serious, just nagging and hurting, but there nevertheless.

And he had to get to that damned Apache now before he got to him. How he wished for his Winchester, stuck useless in its saddle holster on the back of his bay deep in the spruce.

Taut and electrified, he moved swiftly, crouched and running, making a wide arc to come up behind the Apache's last position.

Some hundred yards from it, he paused and slipped fresh shells into the used chambers of his Colt, waited and listened.

Only the scream of an eagle hanging high above him on the updraughts intruded on the stifling air.

Then it came; totally unexpected. A high-pitched song. A death-chant, Maddon knew. The bronco was warning his ancestors he was coming. Or it was a cunning trap . . . ? You never knew with these desert-hardened, cunning fighters.

Maddon moved forward cautiously, hardly daring to breathe in case he missed some tell-tale sound that would warn him of the Apache's approach.

He came upon the buck suddenly. He was sat spread-legged, wedged in a cleft at the base of the boulder he had fired down at Maddon from. Blood from a gaping exit stomach wound fed the dry earth between his bare legs, staining it widely. And Maddon wondered how the buck could sing, his face all ruined the way it was. And why he was sat there, instead of hunting him.

The buck held his Sharps firmly in front of him. Maddon reckoned he was no more than sixteen years of age. They got younger, he thought absently, his thin, strong lips clamping into a stern line.

It was during this thought that the Indian seemed to become aware of Maddon standing there, looking at him.

The song broke off abruptly, and without hesitation, the Sharps came up.

Maddon blasted off immediately. This time he made no mistake. The red headband ripped off to splatter, along with blood and brains and lead, against the rock face behind it.

As if fastened there, the brave stayed, sat upright, wedged against the big yellow boulder. Slowly the Sharps slipped from his fingers to drop onto the ground before him and a kind of peace came to his torn features.

A quick, curious examination of the corpse told Maddon that his second shot had severed the buck's backbone. So that was why he hadn't moved. He must have been paralysed by his shot. And a disabled buck had no future in this land. His death song had been asking Maddon to come and finish the job, if he could.

With faint regret Maddon turned and left the buck sitting there looking blank-eyed across the beautiful land, the spirit of which, so Maddon had heard, the Apaches considered they were so inextricably bound up with — their eternal mother.

Now Maddon blinked. He was still lumbered with another problem. The hombre that had thrown down on him.

As he thought, he moved position again from beside the Apache, melting into the yellow rocks and scrub.

He settled in his new hide, his face grim, and quietened his body and listened to the sighs of the land around him for at least twenty minutes before he moved again — then only after he had satisfied himself it was reasonably safe to do so.

The broncos that roamed these hills were almost certainly escapees from the reservations. And this was their last refuge. They would kill mercilessly to defend it. They had nothing to lose, only their lives. And that, to them, he guessed, was a better option than life cooped up on some soul-destroying reservation.

The great silence of the wasteland had descended again. He rose and edged his way slowly to where he had left the body of the gun-happy hombre and the palomino he had ridden.

The palomino had moved further into the rocks to find food. Flies were now busy feasting upon the man's congealing blood. Maddon caught the horse, unhitched the lariat from the palomino's saddle and heaved the dead body onto its back. Maddon was a big, raw-boned man and the task wasn't too difficult. Unemotionally, he lashed the body to the saddle.

Now he led it to his own bay. He mounted immediately he reached it and pushed off down the long rocky slope falling away towards the flatter, more fertile ground before the mountains further south, trailing the body on the palomino behind him.

He wasn't looking forward to what was awaiting him in Clayton. But it had to be done.

All in all, this day had turned out to be a bad one. And God knew what lay ahead, he thought bitterly.

2

IT was early the following morning Maddon reached Clayton. He had set off two hours before dawn from his overnight camp with the intention of getting the matter that brought him here over quickly. He would then ride on immediately to visit Holly, his wife Jane and his nephew Nathan, and find out what Holly wanted.

He found Clayton to be a large town, sat flat and grey at the southern end of the timber-dotted, brown-green, vast Wassala Valley floor, undulating between the blue mountains north and south of it.

Silver rods of railway lines arrowed in from east to west. Sidings ran into stock pens a mile or so to the west, beyond the town. At the moment the buildings stood forlorn and ghostly in the pink, early-morning sun. He brought his gaze in now to the town station which was crowded on its north side by clap-board shacks and warehouses.

The town was already bustling and alive with riders and wagons, coming and going; storekeepers brushing off their fronts. But the body over the saddle of the palomino trailing behind him on the rope he held caused stares from all directions to follow him. Some curious, some downright amazed, to see the corpse he toted.

Treating them with little heed, he paused and stared at the cowboy who was leaning against a tie-rail outside a saloon that announced it was the Rangeman's Rest. The waddy gawped open-mouthed, first at him, then at the body over the palomino.

"You got law in this town?" Maddon demanded.

For a moment the cowboy remained awe-struck. He seemed stunned that Maddon had stopped to ask him such a question. Then his face twisted up, as though he wasn't hearing right and pushed quickly off the tie-rail.

"Lordy — why you askin' me, Holly?" He waved a hand up the street. "You-all know it's next to the land office."

Maddon paused a moment, about to question the man for calling him Holly before realizing it was a genuine response. He could be taken for Holly very easily, he recalled. As boys they had even fooled their own mother more than once. There was only one thing that really separated them. He was a left hand gun. Holly used the right.

Without commenting, he touched the brim of his black stetson with a horny finger. "Obliged," he said and urged the bay onwards.

At the sheriff's office he dismounted, wrapped rein over tie-rail and clumped onto the boardwalk and into the dim, at present cool, building.

Staring up at him from the paper-littered desk was a pink, round face in which sat two of the bluest eyes Maddon had ever seen. The man had small, elastic lips and a snubbed nose. His sandy hair was greying at the temples, but his body was square and thick-set and his shoulders looked powerful.

The sheriff stared closely at him. "Looks as though you've been doing some ridin', Holly," he grunted. Then he added, a trifle suspiciously, his eyes narrowing, "Say, you look different . . ." After moments, something that suggested enlightenment came to his features. "Yeah, I got it now — you've let your hair grow. And I ain't seen the hogleg on your left hip afore." Then he shrugged, as if it didn't really matter anyhow. "Well, what can I do for you?" he grunted. "Not trouble with the Rowel again?"

Maddon's mind became alert. Trouble with the Rowel . . . again? The sheriff had said it as though it was not an uncommon state of affairs for Holly to be in. However he saw no point in hiding his true identity.

"Ain't Holly," he said. "I'm his

twin — Frank Maddon. And I got me a body outside, sheriff. Want the story?"

With a face that suddenly grew long and eyes that hardened to ice-blue, the sheriff growled abruptly, "Tell it."

The lawman listened intently, his keen look revealing nothing. When Maddon finished, he said,

"An' you don't know the man?"

Maddon shook his head. "He never gave me chance to ask," he informed. "But I found a letter addressed to the Rowel Ranch in his pocket."

At the mention of the ranch the sheriff looked even more closely at him, and an animal wariness came to his features. "The Rowel, you say?"

The lawman rose quickly, enabling Maddon to size him up thoroughly. He reckoned the sheriff could be no more than five feet eight inches in stature, but his shoulders were broad and powerful.

The sheriff reached to a peg behind him and unhooked a brown, high-crowned stetson and pulled it on before he stepped towards the door.

At it he paused, his bright blue eyes questioning. "You got the Apache scalps . . . ? There's a bounty to be had on them."

The revelation digusted Maddon and he let it show. "I ain't that kind of man, sheriff."

The sheriff's gaze appraised him shrewdly before nodding his head. "No . . . I guess not." Then he narrowed his gaze as if remembering something. "Frank Maddon . . . You the hombre who helped Klute Maser clean up Cedar Creek?"

Maddon nodded bleakly. "For reasons personal," he grunted. "It had to be done."

The sheriff stroked his cleft chin gravely and Maddon thought he detected a grim light suddenly appear in the lawman's eyes. "Don't it always?" he enquired tiredly. He stepped outside.

In the rosy morning Maddon found the air was already warming up rapidly. At the sight of the palomino, the sheriff blew a gust of air down his nostrils and stepped off the boardwalk and paced quickly to the man over the saddle.

When he turned to face him again, Maddon could see the sheriff's face had lost its pinkness and his eyes had returned to blue ice. His small lips were compressed.

"My God, Maddon," he said then, quietly, "you've gone and shot Hannibal Mosely's son — Walt."

Because of his ignorance about the hierarchy in Wassala Valley, Maddon didn't appreciate the sheriff's almost whispered declaration, but felt concerned enough by what he had recently learnt about Holly being involved in trouble with the Rowel, to say:

"He shouldn't go pullin' a gun on a man. He should have learnt by now it's usually a fatal mistake."

The small sheriff made a growling noise in the back of his throat and licked his lips. "Maddon," he said seriously, "the Rowel is the biggest spread around here. And Hannibal

Mosely was the most powerful man until he virtually handed the running of the ranch over to Walt, wanting to sit back and enjoy his old age." The lawman blinked, his blue gaze narrow. "You're in deep trouble, whether it was self-defence or not."

Maddon nodded slowly. "Yeah, I'm coming round to figuring as much," he said. "And what I hear, sheriff, Holly's land borders the Rowel, too, don't it?"

The lawman nodded gravely. "And there's been bitter words over it for some time," he informed. "The Rowel disputes Holly's right to some water near the boundary, though it's your brother's sure enough, according to the records filed in the land office. And I've warned Hannibal Mosely about goin' on the prod over it. But he's still actin' mule-headed about it, sayin' Walt's in charge and knows what he's doin', and that he goes along with him." The sheriff glowered at Frank. "Maddon — you've done your brother no favours at all killin' Walt."

Maddon drew himself up to his full height of six-feet two-inches and took out the telegraph that Holly had sent him and offered it.

"Well before you go gettin' ideas on Mosely, sheriff — that I maybe killed him because of the trouble between the Rowel and Holly," he said, "let this explain why I'm here."

The sheriff read the telegraph quickly and grunted. "No mention of the ruckus with the Rowel. Jest that you should get here. From that, I judge you didn't do it because of that."

Maddon nodded. "You judge right."

The sheriff looked at Maddon shrewdly now. "Well, like I said, the horn-lockin' between the Rowel and your brother's spread — the Bar M — is serious. Walt must have mistaken you for Holly and reckoned he was in with a chance to settle it, there and then, once and for all. Walt was reckless enough and foolish enough to try a thing like that."

"He ain't no more," Maddon commented bleakly. For a moment he stood contemplating his left boot, before he said, "So what are you goin' to do about it, sheriff?"

Maddon watched the blue eyes come up and study him. Then the sheriff took off his brown stetson and wiped sweat off his forehead with a large handkerchief before replacing it and replying.

"Nothin'," he said. "You're free to go. A guilty man wouldn't have taken the trouble to fetch in the man he'd gunned down. Atop of that, knowin' Walt, that's the sort of damn-fool stunt he would attempt to pull. Walt's been tryin' to prove for a couple of years now he throws a bigger shadow than Hannibal, particularly since Hannibal more or less turned the ranch over to him. But he doesn't and damn-well knows it — or knew it, since you've salivated him — but was too bull-headed to admit it. And the fact that he didn't sat in his gut like poison."

Maddon nodded, a worm of relief coiling through him that his story had been believed and he was dealing with a square lawman. Out of curiosity he asked, "I didn't catch your name, sheriff."

The blue eyes appraised him once more. "No harm to know," he said after moments. "Wallis Tavener."

Maddon nodded grimly, not surprised at the news. "Braxen County range war," he said, respect growing in him.

That had been a bloody business, he remembered, and Tavener's part in it now legendary. "Makes Cedar Creek look small fry," he commented.

Sheriff Wallis Tavener shrugged. "I want no medals. You get the job done, an' when they don't want you any more, you move on." Again Maddon was aware that the sheriff's blue eyes were studying him speculatively. "I got a bottle inside . . . Want to cut trail dust?"

Maddon nodded eagerly. "Why not?"

he said. "It'll help put what I want to ask you."

Narrow-eyed, Tavener halted in the doorway and appraised Maddon. "An' that is . . . ?"

"I want to take the body of Walt Mosely to the Rowel Ranch," he said. "Explain Holly had nothin' to do with it."

The sheriff gusted out breath. "Hannibal won't listen," he warned.

"He'll have to."

A cynical smile curled Tavener's small mouth. "Hannibal Mosely's never been made to do anything in his life he didn't want to do. He'll make his own mind up. And Walt was his only son. God knows how he'll take it."

Then the sheriff gave him a long look. "I'm coming with you, Maddon," he said then. "As the law in this valley, I have to."

Maddon nodded. "I'd appreciate that, sheriff."

Tavener's eyes remained serious. "I

guess we'd better have that drink. I've a feelin' we're goin' to need it."

★ ★ ★

The ride to the Rowel took them until mid-afternoon, and the trail passed through good cow country, stocked with high quality beeves. Long before they saw the Rowel ranchhouse, they had passed a bunch of riders working cattle through the belly-high grass of some particularly good pastureland. One had detached himself immediately on sight of them and had ridden off north, the way Tavener was taking Maddon.

Maddon found the Rowel stood on rising ground under the foothills of the mountains to the north, which reared majestically behind the long, low building. Around it, Maddon saw large barns, a wind-pump and another long, low structure Maddon assumed was the bunkhouse.

There was already a reception

committee of half a dozen hard-faced rangemen grouped before the long verandah running the length of the solid timber ranchhouse. Some sat on the wooden stairs going up to it, whittling or mouthing chaws or just staring with range-narrowed, suspicious eyes at Maddon and Wallis Tavener.

Tavener eased forward and stared at the men. "I'd be obliged if you'd tell Hannibal we're here," he said to no one in particular.

A tall, painfully thin ranny grunted, "He knows."

Tavener growled and glared at the waddy for a moment before shouting, "Hannibal . . . Wallis Tavener. We got your boy here."

Maddon watched then as the short, powerfully built man with an oddly bland-looking face came through the big door of the ranchhouse and stared with the coldest grey eyes Maddon had ever encountered. And they were fastened on him. The rancher's hand rested on a holstered Colt high on his right hip.

"You kill him, Maddon?" he demanded without preliminaries. His voice was deep and booming.

Frank met the man's piercing stare steadily. "I'm Frank Maddon," he said in clear, calm tones, "Holly Maddon's twin. And I want you to know he had no part in it. Your son pulled a gun on me, Mosely. I had no choice but to kill him. I'm damned sorry, but there it is."

His face impassive, Hannibal Mosely now stepped down off the verandah and walked to the body over the palomino. For a moment, he touched lank, blood-matted brown hair hanging long from it before turning, his body visibly shaking with pent-up emotion. Then his even, harsh voice came through narrow lips,

"What do you think, Tavener? I value your opinion."

The solid sheriff hitched in the saddle. "I figure he's telling the truth," he said firmly. "Walt threw down on him. I'm takin' no action against him."

Mosely now blinked his eyes and licked his lips. "Even so, what is about to be done, has to be done. There's no other way for me."

Maddon narrowed his eyes.

"Meaning . . . ?" he growled.

"I'm going to kill you," Mosely stated baldly, his stare cold and emotionless. "Or you kill me. And I've told my men it's solely my business. If you kill me, you are free to ride on."

Sheriff Tavener's sharp voice cut in, "Now hold on, Hannibal. There's no need for more killin'. Walt was a hot-head and you know it. It was bound to happen sooner or later. It was just Maddon's damned bad luck it fell to him. Damn it, man," grumbled Tavener, "you have responsibilities to the valley. And things aren't settled like this anymore."

Mosely's bland face remained bland and unemotional. "I don't need you to tell me my responsibilities, Tavener.

My son has been killed. My code demands one thing. I, as his father, will avenge his death, or die in the trying."

Tavener's voice now changed, became cold and clear. And he slid his gun out with a suddenness that surprised everybody, including Maddon.

"Back off, Hannibal," he growled. "I can't allow it. Feudin's a dead duck in this valley while I'm sheriff."

Maddon watched Mosely's cold, piercing stare, centred solely on himself, harden even further. It didn't leave him even though Mosely spoke to Sheriff Tavener.

"If you interfere, Wallis," Mosely said evenly, "my men have orders to gun you down."

The small lawman reared in his saddle. "By God, no man threatens me," he menaced harshly. "If you try for Maddon, you'll get it first."

Maddon watched Mosely's chin lift slightly. For the first time, the rancher's stare left him and confronted Tavener.

As it did so, Mosely moved forward, close to the left stirrup of Maddon's plain working saddle. Maddon recognised what could be a heaven-sent opportunity.

"We'll see, Wallis," Mosely was saying. Then he turned hard grey eyes up. "Maddon — I'm backing off and calling you out. Prepare yourself!"

Frank knew he had to move, despite the situation being crazy. He now appreciated a man like Mosely would do exactly what he said.

With fierce speed his left hand pulled his Colt and brought it down on Mosely's head with stunning force. The rancher let out a harsh cry, his gun half-out before he collapsed into a heap and lay still.

Immediately, Maddon swung his Colt onto the now tensed-up rangemen on the steps.

"I want no blood spilt here, gents," he growled. "There's been enough with Walt."

Tavener moved to side him. "Likewise, boys," he said. "Don't start something you can't finish."

Maddon began to sidle his mount backwards. Tavener's own horse matched his step for step. The rangehands slowly rose, staring at them with narrow, alert eyes, hands hovering near their guns.

It was then Maddon saw the glint of something at the corner of the nearest barn. He turned hard eyes to see what it was — a rangeman, his Colt lining up.

Maddon's reply matched the rangehand's. Maddon heard the savage hum of lead pass his head, dangerously close, but the cowboy was staggering back against the barn, his cry of pain sharp, his left hand hugging his damaged right shoulder, his Colt dropping to the ground from his right hand.

Maddon knew the waddy was out of the fight and turned his attention back to the rangehands. Tavener still played his short-barrelled Colt across them, seemingly having sufficient confidence in Maddon to deal with the interruption.

Then Tavener grated, "Remember, boys, Hannibal said that this was his business. You boys had no part in it. If you do try to interfere with our progress, you'll find me a very unforgiving lawman, I promise."

There were a few more moments of tension before a tall, rangy, leather-faced rangeman stepped out of the house. Maddon eyed him and met the man's keen, steely gaze.

"Back off, boys," the stranger said quietly. Then he swung his eyes to the sheriff. "Wallis, you seem too ready to accept this man's story. If he's Holly Maddon's brother — it could have been planned."

Tavener hitched in the saddle. "I know it wasn't. It's more than a gut feelin', Ace. I reckon Maddon wouldn't be here if it was like you suspect. He'd be long gone."

The man named Ace didn't seem to Maddon to be persuaded. "Why?" he growled. "He's probably here to side Holly." His eyes became steely.

"Sooner or later, he's goin' to have to pay for Walt's death, Wallis. You have my word on that."

Tavener narrowed his eyes. Warning crackled in his voice. "If it's done from the bushes then it'll be murder, Ace," he grunted. "And whoever done it will hang. You have my word."

A sneer came to Ace's lips.

"Because you settled one range dispute don't say you can do it again, sheriff," he returned meaningly, his voice harsh and cold. "You ain't as young as you was."

"Don't threaten me, Ace," Tavener ground out. "Keep out of it."

"I'm kin, Wallis," Ace pointed out. "Hannibal's my uncle. Walt my cousin. No way I can walk away from this."

Tavener grunted. "You're a hot gunhand, Ace," he said, "so I've heard. But don't let it go to your head."

The sheriff turned to Maddon now and Frank met his bright, hard blue gaze.

"Let's go, Maddon. Ace'll go along

with Hannibal's order. More so, now he stands to inherit with Walt gone."

That brought an immediately reaction from Ace. "By God, go careful with that tongue of yours, Tavener," he hissed angrily. "Hiding behind that shield ain't certain insurance."

A belly laugh came from Tavener. "Don't feel lucky, Ace," he advised. "Luck don't last forever."

With that Tavener swung his horse and Maddon fell in beside him, his back tingling. He didn't feel as safe as Tavener appeared to feel.

It seemed now this play had to hot up and become downright nasty.

Some half a mile down-trail he turned to Tavener. A few things needed clearing up.

"That's Ace Pedlar, ain't it?" he said. "Recall some years ago, he used to operate around Virginia City, taking all the gold dust he could from the miners. He was called out more than once, accused of dealing a crooked deck. He was fast enough to win all the arguments until Wild Bill ran him out."

Tavener nodded affirmation. "Hannibal affirmed he's kin," he informed, with a cynical tone that wasn't wasted on Maddon. "It figures. He's mean enough to come from that brood. He showed up at the Rowel two months ago, when the trouble with your brother got no nearer solving. I've been holdin' them apart ever since. Holly's been shot at more than once. 'Course, nobody knows who. But it don't take much imagination," Wallis Tavener finished, meaningly.

Maddon spat. "Seems a mighty unhealthy place — Wassala Valley."

Tavener's eyes held his own brown, hard stare. "I'm finding it hard to hold the lid on," he admitted candidly. He looked sourly at Maddon. "And you ain't helped none."

Maddon felt slightly annoyed by the accusation. "Damn it, the man was out to kill me," he protested.

Tavener's face relaxed. "I guess so," he grunted. "I just get mighty weary of it all sometimes."

Maddon lost his aggression and nodded his agreement. "Yeah — I had that feeling more than once policing Cedar Creek," he agreed. "Up a dark alley, back prickling, and your gut taut as fence wire."

A wry smile twisted Tavener's small lips. "Damn it, an' I thought I was the only one who felt that . . ."

They both laughed out loud and Maddon warmed to this squat, tough little lawman.

But the bark of the rifle sent both men spurring forward towards a stand of cottonwoods nearby, lead humming around them like angry bees.

3

ONCE in the cover of the cottonwoods, together they dropped off their mounts and took refuge amongst the trees. Now, pressed up against a tree bole, his breath coming harshly from him, Maddon stared at Tavener.

"What do you think?"

Tavener glanced briefly at him, his blue eyes bright and alert. "Maybe just a scare tactic."

Maddon nodded, holding his bay as she pulled at the reins in his hand. He surveyed the undulating land before them. Then he caught the glint of the sun on metal, and saw the rider spurring swiftly away over a swell in the land above the trees from where he knew the shots had come.

He stared at Tavener. "Follow?"

The stocky sheriff shook his head.

"Ain't worth the sweat."

Maddon silently agreed. Also, he had Holly to see.

"'Bliged if you'd point me towards my brother's place," he said then.

Tavener began to climb into the saddle again. Settled in it, he pointed a short, stubby finger. "Go south-west for three, four miles," he advised, "until you hit the creek." Irony came to his voice. "The one that all the fuss is about. Just follow it until you reach the Bar M."

Maddon slid comfortably into his saddle and tugged rein to steady the skittish bay. Suddenly, he felt a wry humour stirring in him.

"It's been an interesting day, Tavener," he said with a grin that exposed strong, even teeth.

Tavener returned the smile. "You could say that, Maddon." He pushed out a leather-gloved hand. "And I'm Wallis to my friends."

Maddon leaned over and took the sheriff's offered mitt. "Frank to mine," he said warmly.

Tavener spat now. "Thet out of the way," he grunted, narrowing his blue gaze, "what you plan to do now you're here?"

"Find out what Holly needs me for."

"You've guessed that by now," Tavener suggested.

Frank had to agree. He nodded. "Pretty fair idea."

Tavener kept his stare narrow. "I want to keep the lid tight down on this, Frank, if I can," he said, a hint of warning in his voice.

"There'll be no trouble from me, Wallis," he promised. "Less it's forced on me."

Tavener fumbled in his inside coat pocket and took out a silver case. From it he produced two long, slim stogies. He offered one. When they were both lit and blue smoke drifted on the still air between them, he said,

"I've been authorized to swear in an extra deputy while this trouble is on, Frank, in the hope it might impress on the Rowel their antics won't be stood for. I could use a man with experience. How do you feel about it?"

Maddon met the sheriff's candid, enquiring stare, the request taking him aback for a moment. "Can't say I wouldn't be proud, Wallis," he said frankly. "I would."

Tavener gestured eagerly towards Maddon with his hand-held stogie. "How about it, then?" he encouraged. "It runs to fifty dollars a month and found. Ain't much, I know. But look at it this way: it would give your efforts on Holly's behalf more weight if you had a badge to back you up."

The offer was attractive, Maddon had to admit to himself. "Could I leave the decision for a day or two, Wallis?"

"For the right man, I can wait that long." There was no flattery in the sheriff's words.

How Tavener could be so sure he considered him the right man, Maddon wanted to know.

"I could be played out," he suggested. "It happens. Cedar Creek was quite a while ago."

"The way you handled the business at the Rowel told me all I want to know," Tavener said confidently. He eased his horse towards the west, then rested his sincere gaze on Maddon. "See you in two days, Frank?"

Maddon nodded. "One way or the other — two days at the most."

Parting from Tavener, Maddon urged his bay towards the south-west, to pick up the creek running past Holly's place.

★ ★ ★

Maddon became concerned long before he reached the Bar M. The thin, black column of smoke rising into the cobalt sky in the distance in front of him boded ill. He urged the bay into a canter. As the smoke drew nearer, so did the sound of gunfire become apparent.

Fully alarmed now, he left the creek — which took a long loop around the hill before him — and urged the bay up the incline. When he breasted the hill, the slope on the other side fell gently for more than a mile to the low building by the creek. What Maddon guessed was the barn, some hundred yards from the house, was burning furiously.

This had to be Holly's place.

Grim-faced, hunting telescope pressed to his eye, Maddon assessed the situation. Obviously people were inside the ranchhouse. Puffs of powdersmoke came from various places around it. Maddon counted four guns.

Around the house he tallied five guns, firing from the selected cover of corral fences and depressions in the ground. And Maddon knew he had to set up a crossfire of sorts to be of any help to those in the house. A sixth man was behind a third building, holding three horses. Other mounts were tethered to a tie-rail built there.

And it was obvious to Maddon by the body sprawled some twenty yards from the ranchhouse, and the fire burning smokily in front of it, that an attempt had been made to torch the house.

He looked round for cover, to take him closer to the shooting. He felt sure he had not been seen yet. All their concentration had to be centred on the ranchhouse.

He put his glass away in its leather pouch, stowed it in his saddlebags and cast a narrow gaze around the land.

A quarter of a mile east there was a rash of trees and brush arcing down the hillside that, he reckoned, would afford him cover and bring him within about four hundred yards of the action.

He dropped back off the skyline and urged the bay into a loping run. At the trees he took extra caution as he threaded his way down the incline. The only man likely to notice him, he guessed, would be the man holding the horses. And he had his head around the building edge, watching the gunplay raptly.

On the edge of the trees he found a flat boulder that would afford good protection and give him an ideal firing position. Now he tethered the bay back in the timber behind a clump of rocks and moved forward in a crouching run.

His body was tingling slightly now with anticipation for the action. He wiped away the sweat trickling off his forehead and rolling down the side of his aquiline nose. Then he hunkered into position and nestled the Winchester into his shoulder and set the range on the backsight.

It had to be the horse-holder to start with, he thought coldly, clinically. And drew the bead squarely on the man's chest.

His shot cannoned in, drowning out the noise of the shooting around the ranchhouse. And the man with the horses let out a harsh cry as he twisted back, releasing the reins in his hands, letting the three horses he was holding go. Then he was grovelling around the corner of the building, clawing out his Colt, to find cover from Maddon's Winchester, shouting to his sidekicks as he did so.

Heads turned first to the man, then followed his arm pointing to Maddon's position. At the sound of Maddon's gun, the shooting from the ranchhouse hotted up.

Without hesitating, Maddon sighted up on another gunman and squeezed off. It brought a yelp from his target, but no indication of a hit, which disappointed Maddon.

Then the shout came clear from the attackers. "Git to the horses. We've done enough fer now."

It seemed the gunsels needed no prompting and scrambled back through the grass towards the back of the building where four mounts were still tethered, setting up a barrage of lead, both at the ranchhouse and Maddon's position, as they did so.

It was hot enough to cause Maddon to duck as the lead whined viciously off the rock he lay behind and snarled through the trees above him. By the time Maddon felt it safe enough to make his reply, the six men were mounted, two doubled up, the wounded man being held on by a big, burly hombre. Soon, they were kicking flanks away into the screen of trees nearby.

Frustrated, Maddon chased them with more lead, but without success, and lowered his Winchester to his side when he realised he was wasting shot.

It was then he spotted Holly stepping out of the ranchhouse, to shade his eyes against the sun and peer up at his position. It was like seeing himself in the mirror, Maddon thought, they were so alike. Except that Holly had his hair clipped short and had his gun high on his right hip, not low-slung on his left as he had.

He waved, then turned to get his bay. When he reached it, he cased the

Winchester and climbed up. The horse was tired; as he was. They'd covered plenty of miles of late. He knew he would have little chance of making a chase out of it if he followed the gunsels that had just ridden off, even though some were doubled up.

He turned his mount down towards the Bar M.

He could see Jane now and Nathan emerging from the ranchhouse. The boy had grown. He was already taller than Jane.

As he drew rein before the modest house, Holly grinned up at him broadly.

"Allus did have a keen sense of timing, Frank."

Maddon climbed down and took Holly's eager hand. "I can't leave you five years," he mock-grumbled, matching Holly's broad grin, "without you gittin' yourself into some sort of trouble."

Holly nodded. "Yeah — it is all of five years, ain't it? The time jest flies."

Feeling warm inside Maddon turned to Jane. She had streaks of grey in her raven hair now, but she was still a handsome woman and her soft brown eyes lit up to see him. She seemed not to have been troubled by the fracas just now. And the Henry rifle clasped in her hand told of her active part in it.

He pressed her tenderly to him and kissed her gently on her creamy cheek. "You get prettier, Jane, I swear," he said.

She dipped a mock curtsey. "Why, thank you, sir. You always did make a better liar than Holly."

Maddon raised his hands in the form of mock horror. "I don't need to lie to you Jane Maddon and you know it. You know you're as pretty as a picture."

He turned then, to Nathan. His nephew had the gangling body of a boy of fifteen. His face was slightly pimply and his eyes were Maddon eyes, brown and keen, but his firm chin was Jane's. Maddon noticed he held the rifle in his hand with comfortable ease. The boy's hand-grip was strong as it closed round his own.

"Howdy, Nathan!" he greeted. "Damn it you were button-size the last time I saw you."

"Ain't no longer, Uncle Frank," he said with a swell of his chest.

Maddon nodded and patted his shoulder fondly. "You're right there, boy."

Then Mat Fallon, who had been with Holly since his brother had started up the small ranch seven years ago, came out of the house, his Sharp's rifle resting on his broad shoulder. Mat had gone grey since Maddon had last seen him, but his stocky frame appeared to be still strong and giving the impression it was packed full of restless energy.

"Damn it, Mat," Maddon grunted. "You still workin' for this ornery brother of mine?"

"Somebody has to keep an eye on him," commented Mat dryly. He grinned and took Frank's offered hand

and shook it warmly.

Maddon became serious then. "Know the dead man?" he said, nodding at the corpse before the ranchhouse, the torch still smouldering in front of it.

Holly shook his head. "No, but I can guess," he said surely. "Tell you after supper, Frank. Figure our friends won't be back for a spell."

Maddon was hesitant. "What about the barn down there, Holly?"

Holly turned brown eyes at the smouldering skeleton. "It's a loss I can ill-afford, Frank, but there ain't a deal we can do about it now. I'll build again when this business is out of the way."

Maddon nodded, glad to know Holly still met his troubles head on.

★ ★ ★

It was a beautiful sunset.

Maddon watched as the red orb dived below the high hills to the west and the huge valley — spreading vastly before him and Holly — filled with purple shadows. The soft chuckle of the creek full of ice-cold mountain water made it an even more peaceful scene.

Maddon sighed contentedly and patted his stomach. It had been a great meal Jane had laid on; now he and Holly sat on the verandah enjoying their pipes.

"I don't know for sure but I'm almost certain they were Ace Pedlar's men," Holly explained about the gunsels that afternoon. "I figure he has them holed up in the mountains. 'Course, he doesn't claim to know anything about them — " Holly turned and looked seriously at him " — but I'm not a fool, Frank. They only started to function after Ace arrived in the valley. Whether or not Hannibal Mosely knows about them, I'm not sure. But my guess is Walt Mosely sure does."

Warning flashed in Holly's eyes. "Walt's a mean piece of work, Frank," he growled. "I reckon he has ambitions of owning the whole valley an' don't give too much of a damn how he does it. I never had any serious trouble with Hannibal."

Maddon stirred in his chair at the mention of Walt Mosely. He knew it had to be said. "Well, he ain't any more," he grunted.

He went into the story.

After he'd told about the encounter with Walt in the hills east, Holly stared at him, puffing on his short briar pipe fiercely, his eyes round and disbelieving.

"You've shot Walt?" he said, his shock clear in his voice. "That'll set the kite flyin', for sure."

Maddon made a helpless gesture. "He left me no choice, Holly." He growled. "The crazy galoot jest upped his piece an' started shootin'. I reckon he thought I was you. And Wallis Tavener agrees. Anyway, judging by the fracas this afternoon, I'd say the kite's already airborne."

Holly nodded his agreement, the concern on his face melting away to the calm Maddon was used to seeing. "Yeah," his brother sighed. "I guess you're right, Frank." Now Holly narrowed his eyes. "An' Hannibal's threatened to kill you?"

Maddon nodded. "He's made it personal," he bit out. "Man to man — a life for a life. He seems to live by the old feudin' code. I wanted no part of it, nor did Tavener. As far as I'm concerned, Walt asked for it and he got it. For me, that's the end of the story."

"It won't be for Hannibal, Frank," Holly said. "He's a real mean old cuss, but I've allus found him straight. I reckon it's been Walt that's been stirring up all the trouble over this damned creek." Maddon met his brother's now earnest stare. "But it's mine, Frank, an' no amount of threats are goin' to budge me."

Maddon nodded. "Tavener's filled me in," he said. "He agrees it's yours by right, so does the land office."

Holly's brown eyes found his own.

"I could use some help, Frank," he said. "Gun help. Normally, you know I'd fight my own battles — "

Maddon cut in. "Damn it, Holly," he snorted. "Only thing I regret you didn't call me sooner."

Relief seemed to cross Holly's features for a moment. "Guess I should have known. But I'll lay it on the line, Frank. The Rowel has nine rangemen on their books permanent. And Ace has this gang holed up in the hills, I reckon. An' I figure it ain't jest us they want out of the valley. This creek thing is just an excuse to stir up trouble fer me. When I've gone, despite Walt now bein' out of it, I figure Ace'll go after the other smaller ranchers hereabouts, then."

"Yeah." Maddon narrowed his eyes. "What about the other ranchers?" he queried. "Have you approached them? Pointed out to them they could be next?"

Holly nodded, leaned down and tapped out the dottle from the bottom of his pipe. While he inspected the now empty briar he said, "Yes. And they seem to tacitly agree with my opinion." Now Holly shrugged. "But, it's the old story — until they start bein' shot at, they'll figure they'll maybe get away with it."

Maddon grunted again. He'd encountered the head in the sand attitude before. It had never paid off. The strong had always crushed the weak. Like wolves cutting out the young or old or diseased.

Now they lapsed into companionable silence, each man thinking his own private thoughts, until Maddon said, "Wallis Tavener's asked me to swear in as a deputy while this business is sorted out."

Holly's brown eyes swivelled to him. His interest was immediate. "What did you say?"

"Said I'd let him know."

"On my account?"

"Yup."

Holly leaned over and rested his

hand on Maddon's arm. "You gotta take it, Frank," he said. "The stronger the law is, the more it'll make the Rowel think again."

Maddon felt uncomfortable. "I feel I ought to be here, with you, Jane and the boy," he argued.

"Yup, I know you do, Frank, an' I thank you for it," Holly countered. "An', yeah, that's what I had in mind when I asked you here. But we'll make out. An' Clayton is only a dozen miles cross country; fourteen by the trail. We could maybe set up a fire signal tellin' of trouble here at the Bar M if need be . . . But you gotta take the job. When Hannibal sees you are behind a star, he'll maybe back down."

Maddon felt sceptical. And he remembered Ace Pedlar's threat at the Rowel this morning about hiding behind a badge not adding up to much.

"I wouldn't take bets on that, Holly," he said.

"Even so, Frank, I figure Wallis

needs all the help he can get."

Maddon now looked at his brother's sincere face in the yellow light of the oil-lamp coming from the room behind them.

"You seem pretty sure, Holly," he said. "Me, reckon I'll sleep on it first."

Then Holly's look altered, and with a swiftness that surprised Maddon, he felt his brother's horny hand pulling him down below the light of the window.

Holly's voice now whispered tautly, "Somethin' out there, Frank. Could be varmints. But I figure the human kind."

Maddon had heard nothing, and he prided himself on his keen sense of hearing. He shallowed his breathing.

Still nothing.

He stared keenly at his twin now. "You sure, Holly?" he said quietly.

His brother's eyes were narrow, expectant, as he looked out at the dark ground beyond the light. "Near the creek. Heard a hoof scrape."

Maddon knew Holly had shed his Colt for supper, but he . . . well, some men felt naked without, and when you'd sat on a few knife edges . . .

"Stay down," he hissed. "I'll take a look-see."

He slid out the short-barrelled Peacemaker. It was a deadly weapon for near-range, quick-draw work. Then he felt for his Bowie pouched in its sheath at his back. Satisfied it was there, he slid down off the verandah and dropped into the worn grass, bellying down towards the creek, stopping frequently as he got more into the longer grass, to listen.

Then the rider loomed up out of the night. Maddon's eyes narrowed as he recognised Hannibal Mosely heading straight for the ranchhouse. It was then Holly reared up — coming out of the night behind Mosely. And quite suddenly, Maddon wondered how his brother had moved so quickly and silently; wondered why he had been worried about him. Holly moved with more stealth than he did!

"You're covered both ends, Mosely," Maddon called, rising from the grass, the pale light from the ranchhouse giving enough light. "Throw down your hardware. An' don't try your son's crazy trick if you want to live."

Hannibal Mosely stopped his midnight-black stallion, his bland, pale face lengthening. It was then Maddon noticed the bandage under the ageing rancher's ten-gallon.

"I've come to kill you, Maddon," he stated. His face was unemotional. "Be a man and fight me square."

A slow anger began to seep into Maddon. "I gave you my answer to that this morning," he grated. "There's been enough killin'. I'm havin' no truck with feudin'. Your boy brung it on himself."

Mosely's head lifted proudly. "I think not. Defend yourself."

To Maddon's disbelief, Mosely went for his gun. The move seemed to have already been anticipated by Holly. He came charging forward out of the night, leaping and cannoning Mosely out of his saddle. With a harsh grunt, the rancher fell awkwardly, the gun spewing out of his hand. Maddon heard the sickening crack of bone breaking and Mosely cried out with pain.

Now Hannibal Mosely sat up and started moaning and rocking back and forth holding his arm.

Maddon paced forward, holstering his Colt.

"Damn it — what is it with you Moselys?" he growled. "You got a death wish?"

Then he flung to one side when he saw Mosely move quickly and saw the Derringer coming up, gripped in the rancher's good left hand.

4

THE discharge from the Derringer flashed yellow-orange in the starlit night, lancing out of the small gun's snub barrel. Maddon was relieved to hear the lead humming wide.

Feeling really nasty now, Maddon moved in on the feuding rancher, cursing him roundly.

He wrenched the Derringer out of Mosely's hand and threw it into the night, and the rancher let out a harsh gasp.

"My arm," he gasped. "It's broken."

He moaned, in obvious pain.

Maddon snarled icily, "By God, you're damned lucky that's all that is."

Stood nearby, on his feet again after knocking Mosely out of the saddle, Holly said, "I'll get out the buckboard." Then, grudgingly, "We'll have to take him into Clayton. Doc Fredricks'll have to look at that arm."

Still moaning, Mosely protested, "No. Damn it. Take me to the Rowel. I've got a Mex pretty good at settin' bones."

Maddon spat and snorted his disapproval. "Thet outfit's taken enough pot-shots at me, Mosely, of late," he announced. "No, sir. You're goin' to Clayton."

Holly said now with a calm Maddon wasn't feeling, "Guess we can kill two birds with one stone. Take the owlhoot's body in and give Tavener the story."

Maddon nodded his agreement.

With that, Holly left to get the buckboard and Maddon turned his attention to the rancher again.

Mosely had again started to rock back and forth, clasping his right arm, his pale face grimacing against the pain. "Take me to the Rowel," he demanded again. "You'll be left alone. You have my word."

"Thet's what we had this mornin'," Maddon said bitterly. "Yet Tavener and I had to duck lead before we left your stampin' ground."

Mosely's flat, bland face turned up, the cold eyes questioning. The revelation seemed to make him forget his pain temporarily. "Not on my orders," he said fiercely.

"Then your word don't mean a lot around the Rowel these days, Mosely," countered Maddon. He shook his head expressing his disbelief. "An' you got gall comin' here — to my brother Holly's place — when you're doin' your damnedest to run him out."

Mosely's grey eyes tangled with Maddon's own fierce brown stare.

"I've every right to," the rancher returned meanly. "My boy Walt looked it up at the land office and assured me the Bar M was encroaching on our land. Well, I won't stand for that. If Holly admits it and moves his stock off it, that will be the end of it."

Maddon made a disparaging noise, back of his throat. "You mean you didn't check?"

Hannibal Mosely's look was sullen and resentful. "Why should I?" he defended. "Walt was a man grown. His word was good with me. I brought him up to be truthful and straight. But you've sure as hell killed off an old man's dreams of carrying on the line when you shot him down."

Maddon blinked, slightly surprised at the old rancher's revelation. It just could be true, he didn't know the land was legally Holly's. But bitter resentment stirred within him again at being held responsible for Walt Mosely's death.

"Mosely, I hate repeatin' myself, but your boy brought it on himself," he said harshly. "An' that's the damned truth — somethin' Walt was mighty thin with, it seems."

He glared moodily at the rancher. "I reckon, while you're in town, you'd better check with the land office as to who the creek down there belongs to. I guess you're in for a surprise."

For the first time in Maddon's stormy acquaintance with the rancher Mosely looked uncertain, hesitant, as if not altogether disbelieving Maddon.

"I admit," he said, though he appeared loath to say it, "I was a bit shook when Walt told me about the creek. I thought I was fully acquainted with every bit of land belonging to the Rowel." His cold gaze came up, defiantly engaging Maddon's. "But the Rowel is a big spread. I could have just missed it."

"Well it seems you didn't miss it — just forgot it weren't yours," snapped Maddon. "And you didn't even listen to Wallis Tavener when he warned you. I think Walt and Ace, if I read the situation right, have been doin' a lot you don't know about. Ace had his gunhawks here today, shootin' hell out of the ranchhouse and firin' Holly's barn."

Something akin to bewilderment came into the old man's features before they set into a hard, doubting mask. "Ace . . . gunhawks . . . what are you sayin', Maddon?"

"I'm sayin' Walt and Ace were in cahoots and had, until Walt bought it, one aim in mind: to make all the land in the valley Rowel-owned. And not givin' a damn how they did it."

Now Mosely sat, shaking his head. "It can't be true." He sounded shocked, uncomprehending. "Can't be. I brought Walt up good. He wouldn't lie to me, his own father."

At that moment Jane came to the ranchhouse door, sided by Mat Fallon who had his big Walker Colt out and ready. When she saw Maddon she demanded, "Who's that, Frank? What was the shooting about?"

"Hannibal Mosely, Jane," Maddon called. "The damned fool came to call me out an' busted his arm instead. When Holly's rigged up the buckboard I'm takin' him to the doc's in Clayton."

Maddon heard, as he was speaking, Mosely was mumbling to himself, "I brought Walt up good. He wouldn't do that."

Scorn filled Maddon now. In reply he growled, "Maybe you did, I don't know — an' to be sure, I don't care. But I sure know one thing: Ace Pedlar's scum. It don't say much for you to harbour him."

Mosely blinked balefully at him. "Walt seemed to hold him in high regard," he defended fervently, then winced and gasped with pain.

When he'd recovered he said, "He was my sister's boy. Must say I never took to Sam Pedlar, the boy's father. And there's something not straight about Ace. To be frank, I don't like him. There's something I don't trust."

Just then, from the night, Maddon heard the scrape of wagon wheels as Holly drove the buckboard towards the rancher and Maddon.

Maddon was quietly surprised Hannibal

Mosely was being suddenly so forthcoming about his family, especially to himself. Was it that Mosely had already begun to suspect things were not right at the Rowel and Maddon's revelations lent credence to his suspicions, and he was now arguing it out aloud with himself despite Maddon, the shock of his broken arm loosening his tongue, too?

Maddon didn't dwell on finding answers about Hannibal Mosely. His brood had given him and Holly enough trouble already — and the rancher had come here with the intention of killing him.

As Holly drew the buckboard alongside them, he said, "I've put the owlhoot's body in the back, Frank."

Maddon nodded then ordered, "Git up, Mosely."

The rancher grunted harshly as he came to his feet. Now his pale face was ashen and deep pain-lines etched it.

Maddon watched with pitiless eyes as the rancher struggled painfully to pull himself into the buckboard seat.

Settled, Mosely looked deeply at him for moments before firming his lips into a determined line. On the seat, he sat still, staring straight ahead into the night, his face grim.

"Keep your gun on him, Holly," Maddon requested. With that he moved inside the house and picked up his Winchester. Jane caught his arm as he moved out. "Be careful, Frank," she said. Maddon was touched to see the concern in her deep, soft, brown eyes.

He pecked her on the cheek. "Count on it, Jane," he said with a small grin.

Back at the buckboard, out of earshot of the rancher, Holly said, "Want me to ride with you, Frank?"

Maddon shook his head. "I'll handle it, Holly," he said. He mirrored Holly's steady gaze. "I guess I'll take up Wallis Tavener's offer. Maybe a badge will give us more weight. Hannibal doesn't seem to know what's been goin' on."

Holly nodded. "I've half-guessed it,"

he agreed. "We lived peaceable enough before he turned the runnin' of the ranch over to Walt."

Nathan had just finished tying up Mosely's black stallion to the tail-gate and now stood gangling-limbed by it.

Maddon ruffled his hair. "Be seein' you, boy."

Nathan grinned a pimply grin. "Sure, Uncle Frank."

Up on the seat beside the subdued rancher, Maddon clicked the roan between the shafts into life and trotted it into the night.

★ ★ ★

The trail to Clayton was well-worn and easy to follow. Hannibal Mosely sat silent beside Maddon hugging his injured arm, his hard eyes staring into the starlit night. Maddon was thankful for it and pushed the roan in the shafts hard.

Clayton, even at this late hour, was bustling as he drove the buckboard down the wide main street. The tinkle of honky-tonk pianos filled the air. Lights from the saloons and eating premises, plus lights hung on poles lining the thoroughfare, lit the night with a yellow glow. Passing the Theatre Palace, Maddon could hear the trills of a fair feminine voice.

Outside the sheriff's office, Maddon drew rein and looped them round the brake staff.

"This isn't Doc Fredricks', Maddon."

Hannibal Mosely's first words since leaving the Bar M startled Maddon momentarily.

"I've got an attempted murder to report, besides reportin' the raid on Holly's place an' the dead body it produced," Maddon growled. He glared. "You came to the Bar M to kill me, remember, Mosely?"

The rancher's cold grey eyes glinted with sudden fierceness. "I came to call you out, fair and square."

"I don't want to be called out," hissed Maddon nastily. His brown eyes gleamed, the only thing showing the controlled anger within him. "I don't want no part of your crazy feudin' mentality, you hear?"

He spat sourly and glowered at the rancher. "Git down!"

Ignoring Maddon's stern request, Mosely called, "Wallis — you in there?"

Maddon was just about to step forward and drag the rancher out of his seat when Tavener came to the door of his office.

The short, solid sheriff stared first at Mosely, then at Maddon. His eyes narrowed.

"What gives, Frank?" he demanded.

"Holly had his barn burned down this afternoon by a gang Holly claims Ace Pedlar has in the hills," Maddon announced. "One of the gang was shot dead. He's in the back of the buckboard."

"And Hannibal?"

"Came to call me out," Maddon growled economically. "Got a busted arm for his pains."

Tavener turned angry blue eyes on the rancher. "Damn it," he snorted. "I ain't standin' for it, Hannibal."

Mosely's eyes were cold and steady as they met the sheriff's fierce gaze. "I buried my only boy this afternoon, Wallis," he said. "No matter what — me an' Maddon have to see each other through gunsmoke."

Tavener's head craned forward on its thick, bull-like neck. "You're gettin' to be a silly old man, Hannibal," he grated. "Thought I'd made it plain I won't stand for it, d'you hear?"

Mosely's cold grey eyes blinked. "I've lived by the law, Wallis, always have," he said, "you know that. But some things, in my book, go beyond and I won't bend on them."

Tavener let out an exasperated sigh and glowered at the rancher. "Damn it, get out of my sight, Hannibal!" he raged.

Mosely stiffened. "Don't talk to me like that, Tavener; I ain't some range bum you're talking to," he said harshly. "I could get you stripped of that badge." Tavener grinned mirthlessly, his small, elastic lips stretching across his round, pink face. "I got two years to run, Hannibal," he said quietly. "And threats I don't like. Step out of line and I'll run you in so fast your feet won't touch. Hannibal Mosely, or no Hannibal Mosely. Now git!"

Mosely's stare was bald and icy as he climbed, gasping his pain, out of the buckboard seat, unhitched his black stallion and walked erect with it into the night.

The stocky sheriff turned to Maddon now, his voice calmer. "Frank, ride with me down to the undertakers, help me with the body? Fill me in on the way down there."

When they were seated and Maddon had geed-up the roan in the shafts, Tavener said, "Thought any more about my proposition, Frank?"

Maddon nodded. "It's 'yes', Wallis."

Tavener's already relaxed face took

on a satisfied look. "Well, that's something good out of a bad day," he commented.

Studiously now Wallis heaved out his fancy case and offered Maddon a stogie. When both men were well-lit and blowing blue smoke, the sheriff spat,

"Now, what's this business at the Bar M?"

"Rode right into it, Wallis," grunted Maddon.

He told the story.

When he finished Tavener growled,

"I've been havin' rustlin' trouble with that nest of snakes. But I didn't know they were tied in with Ace Pedlar and Walt Mosely. Thought they were some trash out of the Nations. Can Holly prove it?"

Maddon had to shake his head. "I surely don't think so, Wallis," he admitted. "But Holly ain't a man to dream things up. Anyway I got to return the buckboard and pick up my possibles and bay in the morning so

I'll ask him how and what he knows. If he's got backin' proof, though I suspect it's just a hunch — well, we could be in business."

Tavener grunted beside him. "It's goin' to take provin'."

The sheriff's keen stare quizzed him now. "An' you think you went some way to convincin' Hannibal Walt had been lyin' to him?" he said incredulously. "I sure as hell couldn't."

"I sowed some doubt about Walt's impeccability," Maddon stressed with a degree of certainty. "Even though it stuck in Mosely's craw to admit, even to himself, his son was a liar, I got the feelin' he'd been none too happy for a while about the way things were bein' run at the Rowel."

Tavener nodded. "He sure doted over Walt. Where he could soon read any other galoot quick enough, when it came to Walt that sonofabitch could do no wrong. Hannibal just had blinkers on when it came to his boy."

Then the sheriff nudged Maddon

and pointed to the dark maw off to the right. "Turn up that street, Frank," he said. "Tobias Fern — he's the town undertaker and carpenter — has his workshop up there."

Maddon found it was a much more dimly-lit road, little more than an alleyway. It took the width of the buckboard but with only about four feet each side to spare.

They hadn't got a dozen yards into it when the rifle opened up. Lead snarled angrily off the ironwork around the seat and Tavener gasped as he rolled off the buckboard, Maddon following, Winchester gripped firmly in his left hand.

Three more shots splattered the boards of the butcher's behind them. Maddon, keened up now, got the Winchester working, picking out a target in the middle of the roses of fire glaring in the night up the alley.

Tavener's Colt got to talking too. The sound of their gunfire savaged the starlit night as they both opened up.

As if by unspoken agreement, both men ceased firing together and listened intently to the night, the sound of their guns still reverberating through the town.

Then the clatter of hoofs pattered into the night from the direction the gunfire had come from.

"What do you think, Wallis?" Maddon breathed. Tavener growled beside him. "I don't know," he said. "But I'm getting all-fired sick of bein' shot at. Somebody's goin' to have to start payin'."

"They tryin' to soften us up?" Maddon offered.

"They sure as hell are lousy shots if they ain't," growled the lawman. "We must have been silhouetted big as barn doors against the main street lighting. Having said that," Tavener continued wryly, "give me your arm, Frank. Help me into the buckboard. I've got hit in the leg. Don't think it's serious, but it sure as hell is sore."

Surprised at the admission, for the

small, blocky sheriff hadn't made a whimper, Maddon put his right arm under Wallis's armpits. With difficulty, for, despite his small size, Tavener was a heavy man, he got him settled into the seat again.

Following Tavener's terse directions through the town, Maddon drew the buckboard up in front of a neat, white-painted clapboard house in the quieter residential part of the town. A shingle swung creaking in the slight breeze. Dr Lemuel Fredricks MD, was the legend on it.

Light shone through the curtains drawn across the bay window to the right of the blue front door. It must be Hannibal Mosely getting his arm set, thought Maddon, for the big black stallion belonging to the rancher stood hip-shot at the iron jockey stood outside the gate, the reins tied through the steel hoop.

His arm supporting Tavener, Maddon managed to get him to the door and hammered on it.

"Be right with you," came the deep voice from within.

After moments the door opened and Maddon saw a tall, painfully thin man with a white apron over his black broadcloth trousers, pink shirt and plain waistcoat framed in the light from the house. Dr Fredricks' gaunt face was full of hollows and his black eyes questioned Tavener.

"Sheriff . . ." The doctor's gaze flicked momentarily to Maddon before turning back to Wallis. "I heard the shooting . . ."

"Hit in the leg, Lemuel," grunted Tavener. "Be obliged if you'd fix it."

"Sure, sure, come in."

Doc Fredricks stepped back, opening the door wide, and Maddon eased Wallis in and followed Fredricks down the hallway and into the big room off to the left.

Maddon narrowed his eyes. Hannibal Mosely was stood by a narrow, flat table with a sheet over it. His coat was hung loosely over his shoulders, his arm splinted and strapped tight against his chest.

"You know who they were, Wallis?" demanded Doc Fredricks. Then he waved his arm. "Could you climb up onto the table, sheriff, and slip your pants off?"

Tavener grunted with pain as Maddon helped him onto the table. Between them they stripped off the corduroy trousers and long-johns. The wound was a savage groove across the thick rear flesh of the sheriff's calf and seeping some blood.

In answer to the doctor's remarks, Tavener, his face now paled with pain said, "No. They just took pot-shots until it got too hot for them. I don't think this wound was on the agenda . . ." He stared at Hannibal Mosely. "You know anything about it, Hannibal?"

The rancher's face, etched with pain-lines, opened and flushed with sudden anger. "Damn it, Wallis," he growled. "Why should I? I don't have men shooting from alleys."

"The Rowel seems to be at the back of most of the gun activity in the valley of late," insisted Tavener. "What can I think?"

Mosely's cold grey eyes flashed. "You've no proof, Wallis. It doesn't do for an officer of the law to make wild accusations."

"Then you're sayin' we weren't shot at yesterday afternoon, out at the Rowel?"

Mosely's bland face stiffened. "I intend to put an end to that forthwith. Soon as I've checked at the land office concerning the disputed ground between the Rowel and the Bar M I shall be riding home. If it proves to be Rowel land — " Mosely turned cold, narrow eyes onto Maddon " — I expect Holly to have his stock off it within two days."

Maddon held the rancher's cold stare with an equally frosty look. "And if it is Bar M land . . . ?"

Mosely lifted his head proudly.

"Then I will apologise." Now the rancher's eyes grew cold again. "But the other matter between us, Maddon, stands."

Maddon's gut tightened and nasty anger tensed him. "Damn it, man," he hissed. "I've told you I'll have no part of it!"

Mosely remained implacable. "Soon as I'm healed up, I'll be calling you out!"

Maddon drew up to his full six feet two inches and towered over the cool, bland rancher. "Then damn you to hell, Mosely, because that's where you'll go."

Mosely nodded, a faint smile now playing on his lips. With his good hand he settled his stetson over his bandaged head.

"Send me the bill, Lemuel," he grunted curtly and left the room.

Maddon beat his thigh. Dust sprang from it. "Damn the bull-headed fool," he raged.

Wallis grunted. "By the time he's

healed up," he offered, "maybe he'll have cooled down."

Maddon snorted. "That sonofabitch . . . ?" The rest he left unsaid.

Doc Fredricks said then, in surprised tones, "I take it you aren't Holly."

Anger still boiling in Maddon's gut, he took seconds to quell it before answering, "Twins. I'm Frank Maddon."

He shook the doc's extended hand. That over, the sawbones turned to Tavener. "It's going to sting some when the iodine bites in, Wallis," he warned.

The sheriff grunted impatiently. "Get on with it, Lemuel," he growled. "We got work to do. Just patch me up."

5

MADDON was just finishing breakfast at Sarah Wallace's Eatery.

Wallis Tavener had recommended it to him at three o'clock that morning, when the lawman, pale with pain, had sworn him in in the gloomy sheriff's office. The night-duty officer, deputy sheriff Marty Collins, had stood witness.

Maddon belched now, his stomach uncomfortable, and squinted through the steam-streaked glass pane in the door at the early morning sun. Warm, pale rays hit the clapboard buildings of the side street the hashhouse was on, mellowing the weathered timber.

As he looked, Maddon tensed, his chin suddenly jutting with aggression to see Hannibal Mosely appear there. Damn the man, his thoughts raged.

Lacking sleep and now downright annoyed by the rancher's abrupt appearance, Maddon slid out his Colt as Mosely entered the building. Without looking right nor left, the rancher moved straight towards his table.

"Don't start anything," Maddon warned through bear-trap lips. "I'm through playin' with you, Mosely!"

The rancher's bland face was expressionless; the grey eyes cold as dead fish as they appraised him. "Walt lied to me, Maddon," he announced then. "I'll be over to apologise to Holly as soon as I can."

Without another word, Mosely turned and left the eatery.

Maddon got to his feet, slightly taken aback by the rancher's flat, simple statement. Warily he watched Mosely step into the street and request the assistance of a waddy stood nearby, to help him climb onto the back of his big black stallion. Wincing he took up the reins with his free left hand.

Then, his face drawn with pain and void of emotion, Mosely rode off into the yellow-glowed morning without a backward glance.

Maddon blinked and slid his Colt back into leather. He thought, mildly surprised: Just like that? It couldn't be that simple. But he had a gut feeling Mosely meant what he said — he would apologise to Holly. But Maddon also knew, the other business between himself and the rancher was not over and wouldn't be until one of them lay dead. And that was something else.

Maddon glowered after Mosely. Well, hombre, he thought, I'll be long gone. Holly don't need me now. And if you follow me, I'll shoot you down like a dog. That's how personal I feel about your damned feuding ways. And if that leather-slapping kin of yours, Ace Pedlar, follows — he'll get the same.

He set his strong jaw in a determined line, pulled on his worn stetson, and nodded to the middle-aged, motherly-looking owner of the eatery as she came bustling in with ham and eggs for a patiently waiting rangeman.

"Mighty nice meal, ma'am," he grunted, with a pleasantness he wasn't feeling. "A good day to you."

"See you again, mister?" the woman called.

"Maybe, maybe," he grunted. "If you don't, it won't be nothin' to do with the food."

Maddon stepped out into the cool morning air and moved up the boardwalk toward the sheriff's office. Something inside was niggling him. Something didn't feel right here. Perhaps that was what was disturbing his gut?

Something was telling him it wouldn't be a matter of just resigning as deputy sheriff now the land business was settled, riding down to Holly's and passing on Mosely's acknowledgement that there had been a mistake; that Mosely intended to come to the Bar M to personally apologise; that the business between the Rowel and the Bar M was over.

No, there was something else. But he could not put a finger on it. It was just an uneasy feeling. A scratching hunch gnawing at him — that Holly, as well as himself, still had troubles to face.

As he entered the law office, deputy Marty Collins looked up from the report book he was writing in, placed on the desk before him. Surprise came to the lawman's rugged face as his grey eyes appraised him.

"Hello, Frank," he grunted. "You're early."

Maddon growled. "Couldn't get comfortable on them straw bales down at the livery stable."

Collins' surprise lingered.

"You mean Wallis didn't invite you home?"

The question reminded Maddon of Tavener's apology as they had stepped into the cool, early morning dark after the swearing in.

"Said he had a house full. Said he had folks stayin'. His sister and her husband and two children."

Collins nodded his dark head, his grey eyes tired.

"Yeah, that's right," he said. "But you could have knocked up one of the boardin' houses."

Maddon shrugged and settled down in the chair at the rough table in the other corner of the office. Now he was slightly troubled with indigestion, damn it.

"I looked in on Holly's roan," he explained. "The straw bales were there an' looked invitin'. Guess that was all there was to it."

Collins grinned and nodded. "Yup. Know the feelin'. Any damned place when you're tired, eh?"

Maddon crinkled eye corners and looked at the deputy. "That's the size of it." He squinted and kept his gaze on the law officer. "You go, Marty," he offered. "I'll mind the store."

Collins had appreciation written all over his rugged face. "Well, that's wide of you, Frank, it surely is," he said.

"But Wallis is a stickler about a man doin' his stint."

Maddon raised his dark brows and accepted that Tavener could be like that. "Well, I don't want to step on any corns," he said. "Jest thought it social to suggest it, seein' as how I'm here."

Collins' grin stayed. "Don't think it ain't appreciated, Frank."

Maddon nodded tiredly. "Sure, Marty."

He folded his arms and closed his eyes and wished for a peppermint. The deputy returned to the report he was writing up.

★ ★ ★

Wallis Tavener came into the office about 8 o'clock, his eyes puffed with sleep.

"Everythin' all right, Marty?"

"Quiet as the grave."

The sheriff turned to Maddon, now snoring in the chair and cocked a sandy eyebrow at Collins. "How long has Frank been here?"

"About an hour," offered the deputy. "Said the straw at the livery barn was none too comfortable."

"Didn't he find a boarding house?"

Marty raised dark brows. "Didn't want to bother anybody at that time of night."

Wallis grunted. "Guess he could have used the parlour settee at home but I figured he'd want a bed." Tavener cleared his throat. "Well, if you've written-up, Marty, might as well get on home."

Deputy Collins rose from the desk and pressed on his low-crowned grey stetson. "Coffee's simmerin' in the back."

Wallis grinned. "Good to hear. See you tonight, Marty."

"Sure," the deputy said at the door before he went out into the sunlit street.

With the talking Maddon stirred, opened his eyes and got to his feet, happy to find his stomach had settled down again. "Howdy, Wallis!" he greeted. "Leg healin'?"

Tavener nodded his greeting and said, "Just a sore nuisance, is all." Then a smile stretched his small mouth. "You still got straw on your back, Frank. Guess I'll have to brush you down out in the yard. Can't have my officers lookin' like tramps."

Maddon grinned at Wallis's humour before he got to what he'd really come about.

"That aside, Wallis, guess I'll be the shortest servin' peace officer there's ever been," he said then. "Mosely admitted this mornin' the Rowel were wrong. He'll be apologisin' to Holly first chance he has. So I guess that makes me redundant."

Maddon waited for the tough little lawman's reaction.

Tavener raised clear blue eyes to meet Maddon's tawny look, his face long with surprise. "The hell it does, Frank," he countered. "Ace Pedlar's the hombre in my sights." He squinted. "You say Holly suspects that bunch of owlhoots in the hills to be Pedlar's gunsels. Well, I've thought on that last night and it fits the jigsaw. We got to flush them out an' Pedlar. An' there's another thing, too. I figure Ace is aimin' to take over the Rowel, sooner rather than later."

Maddon nodded, his own private thoughts on the matter concurring almost exactly with Wallis's assessment.

He'd come fresh to this situation. And sometimes when a man did that he could see clear through the trees to open ground. And it was looking very much that way to him, too. In fact he'd go further than that: he reckoned Hannibal Mosely could be a target in this. As Wallis had pointed out, Ace stood to inherit now.

He looked at the small lawman thoughtfully. "Has Mosely any other kin, Wallis?"

Tavener shook his head. "None that I know of." Then he waggled it even more positively. "No, I'm sure of it."

Maddon made his mind up swiftly with that news.

"Okay, Wallis, seein' as you ain't amenable to me quittin'," he said, "I'd be mighty interested myself to chase down those owlhoots and see what is under other stones in Wassala Valley."

Tavener nodded, as if he already knew what Maddon's reaction would be. "That's the voice I expected to hear." He smiled. "Once a lawman, always a lawman."

Maddon decided now he had to be down-the-line honest with Wallis. "Well, lately I've hunted men for the bounty on their heads," he admitted. "But I ain't ashamed of that."

Tavener's blue gaze held his. "There ain't a coat of paint difference sometimes, Frank," he said. "I reckon you're a man who'd do the job clean an' straight."

Maddon nodded, satisfied with the answer. And, even as they had talked a plan had formulated in his mind. He eyed the sheriff, now hanging his stetson on the peg behind the swivel chair.

"What do you reckon to this idea, Wallis?" he offered. "I got to take Holly's buckboard back out and pick up my possibles. And, I guess, he needs the roan. What I figure is to try and pick up the trail those gunsels left yesterday. Maybe it'll lead us to some of the stuff we're lookin' for. How about it?"

Tavener's satisfied smile spread across his pink face and he drew out his silver case and offered a stogie.

"You got time for a coffee first, ain't you, Frank?" he asked. Then he frowned and warning came to his eyes. "But no heroics," he advised. "We got men in Clayton willin' to ride posse, if called upon."

Maddon gave him a hurt look. "Damn it, I ain't a fool, Wallis."

★ ★ ★

Maddon found Holly mowing grass in a pasture off the Clayton trail a mile or so from the ranchhouse, and he drew the roan in the shafts to a halt. As soon as Holly saw him he, too, tied rein and climbed off the mowing machine and moved towards him.

The relief showed clear in Holly as Maddon told him the news that Mosely intended to apologise. Then he gave a satisfied nod with his head and a slow smile formed on his lips.

"You get things buzzin' this fast wherever you go?" he demanded.

Maddon grinned. "Bit slow on this one, Holly," he countered.

Holly guffawed before his face sobered and became serious. "You gotta stay on, Frank," he said then, his sincerity clear. "It's good to have you around."

"For awhile, I guess," Maddon said. "But for the moment I figure to try an' look for any sign those owlhoots may have left yesterday. That gang could spell real trouble."

Holly squinted up into the sun to

see him. "Guess you're right there," he agreed. "Want me along, Frank?"

"Lawman's chore, Holly." Maddon nodded to the pasture, enjoying the sweet scents of the new-cut grass. "That's a rancher's." He smiled warmly at his brother. "Thanks for the offer, though."

Then he looked quizzingly at Holly. "One other thing: what gives you the feelin' Ace Pedlar's tied up with the owlhoots?"

Holly rubbed his nose. "They appeared soon after he did," he ventured. "But it's just a hunch, I guess."

"Well, you're not the only one with that gut feelin'," Maddon assured. "I go along with it, too, so does Wallis Tavener."

He touched his stetson with a long finger. "I'll be seein' you, Holly." With that he urged the roan in the shafts into a canter.

At the ranch Nathan took the buckboard and Jane greeted him warmly at the door. While he saddled the bay and secured his possibles, she cooked him ham and eggs. About noon, after farewells, he led off to hunt for tracks.

He was lucky almost immediately. He followed the line he had seen the owlhoots take yesterday afternoon. The trail went through lush meadowland, and crushed grass showed a track a blind man could follow. But Maddon knew, once the gunsels had made their first dash, they'd take a lot more pains over covering their trail.

And the assumption proved true. Sign became as scarce as hens' teeth and he had to pause frequently. In the rough country the owlhoots had clearly deliberately moved into he had to quarter the ground before he picked up the trail again. And all the time he was climbing steadily through the foothills and towards the white-tipped mountains south of the ranch.

Caution began to ride with him now. He could be getting close. And they would almost certainly have lookouts.

Frequently, taking pains to avoid the glint of the sun on his hunting glass, he scanned the hills ahead for any hint of life. A movement . . . a glint of sun on metal . . . a campfire . . . anything.

By late afternoon he was moving up a pine-choked ravine that cut into the mountains, reducing his progress drastically. He found he had to frequently move down to the roaring river that rushed through its bottom to make headway, just as the men he was following had done. But the sign had perked up again. Disturbed pine needles made the tracking easy and it seemed the owlhoots were feeling safe.

The cold soon made him shuck into his sheepskin coat, woolly side in. Above him the sun glared white off the peaks, spearing the blue sky above the pines.

By evening he was out of the ravine, the trail taking him high up into the mountains. Behind him, beyond the pines and foothills, Wassala Valley spread away northwards, the green already deepening into purple, silver-streaked shadows as twilight closed in.

He had to be getting near to the owlhoots, he reasoned. They would have to stay within striking distance of the valley. From all accounts they were active rustling stock as well as hassling Holly.

He fed the bay from his oat sack, then groomed it and hobbled it. By the time the chore was done it was dark and the velvet night was pierced with stars so bright Maddon thought he could reach up and touch them, they appeared so close.

He couldn't risk a fire. He patiently unrolled his trail blanket and wrapped it round him and gratefully chewed on the beef and bread Jane had pressed on him before leaving Holly's place, washing it down with sips of water. But all the time he shivered despite the blanket and the sheepskin coat, his thoughts complaining, some damned country this. Roasting one day, freezing the next!

He was making ready to hunker down to sleep when he spotted the faint, yellow-orange flicker of light blooming out of the darkness on the hillside across from him. It was maybe two miles or more ahead, but definitely a campfire of some sort. He'd put money on it.

He forgot the cold immediately and reached out for his hunting glass. He couldn't see much. The camp was screened with trees. But it was a camp. And it was odds on, the owlhoots' lair.

He saddled the surprised bay and put her into a walk towards the campfire.

It took him the best part of an hour to negotiate the rough incline from his camp to the base of the saddle in the hills and move up the other side towards the fire. But to get close enough he had to move up on foot the rest of the way, the slope too steep, the trees too dense. Now he was getting close enough to hear an upsurge of faint, boisterous talk and laughter before it died down again and was lost.

Almost immediately following it a pack of timber wolves set up a chorus of howling. Maddon's blood curdled although he realised they were far away — deep in the mountains south of him.

He paused frequently now, looking for a watchman. He was relieved to find the gunsels felt confident enough to camp without one. And he was close enough to see the cabin, the corral, the big campfire and the men sat around it passing a jug.

Then he saw the man who had held the horses at Holly's — the one he had put lead into. The owlhoot was propped against a tree bole, jug in his hand, bandaged and looking mighty sick.

Maddon decided he'd seen enough. Stealthily he moved back, got his horse and moved to his previous camp and waited for dawn. Come daylight he'd need to mentally tag landmarks to give him a clear idea of the location of the camp before moving on into Clayton to give Wallis the news.

★ ★ ★

Maddon awoke before dawn next morning, numb with cold, and spent five minutes stamping around and rubbing life into his chilled limbs. He began to wonder if he was getting old, or soft, but decided, miserably, it was just plain cold up here.

After finishing the rest of Jane's bread and beef he settled back against a tree bole and lit his pipe, the blue smoke mingling with the white, condensed breath pluming from his mouth. Frost sparkled like diamonds on the vegetation around him.

In the pre-dawn pearly light he saw fire-smoke rise from the hideout, and it interested him. They were stirring early.

The sun's rays were orange-yellow

on the high white peaks when he saw the gunsels come riding out of the clearing their cabin was in. They zig-zagged single file down the side of the mountain, then ascended up the other side, straight towards him.

Tense, Maddon pulled back and took the reins of the bay — already saddled and loaded and ready for moving.

He pulled back into the trees. After getting three hundred yards off-trail, and above it, he hunkered down to wait.

This could be even more than interesting. Then, naggingly for a moment, Tavener's stricture echoed in his ear, 'no heroics'. He narrowed his eyes. Well, this was gathering information. Nothing heroic about it. In any case, he still felt too cold to be a hero.

They were a hard bunch, that was immediately obvious. Rough, unshaven men, armed to the teeth.

Maddon held the muzzle of his bay.

He didn't want her calling just at the moment.

The wounded one had clearly stayed in camp. Maddon was sorely tempted to ride up and take him as soon as the gunsels were past him, but something held him, telling him that following the men now sullenly passing him would prove more fruitful.

Allowing them ten minutes, he mounted and slotted in behind their trail.

Two hours later, on a completely new trail to the one that had led him to them, the owlhoots halted in the rocky foothills. They began stripping recently-cut pine branches away from a recess in the rocks. He was surprised to see a wagon backed into it. It was very cleverly hidden. Maddon rubbed his chin, eyes narrow. And the question nagged: Why . . . ?

Maddon extended his hunting glass and watched with growing curiosity.

One of the gang dismounted, climbed over one of the sides into the open flat back. He raised one of the bottom boards, then looked up and nodded to the others before replacing the plank and rejoining them.

Then Maddon saw the new rider threading up to where the owlhoots were gathered. It was Ace Pedlar.

6

MADDON narrowed his eyes and set his thin lips in a grim line.

Well, this was as he, Wallis and Holly had suspected, he thought, and enjoyed the satisfaction it gave him. But he hadn't expected this stroke of luck — firm confirmation.

Maddon watched as Pedlar joined the gunsels. It was obvious he ruled the bunch. And the first thing he did was to check the back of the wagon, then immediately ordered it covered again. After more parleying, the owlhoots split up. Ace rode back down the trail he had come up and the gunsels came straight towards Maddon.

Still elated by his good fortune, Maddon dropped below the hill line he had been bellied on and ran for the bay tethered in the trees.

Again, he got off the trail and into cover and waited for the gunsels to pass him.

One thing he did know: he had to see what was in the wagon.

When they passed him the owlhoots were a relaxed, joking bunch this time, their raucous laughter echoing into the mountains.

Seems like it had been a satisfactory meet, Maddon thought bleakly.

After fifteen prudent minutes, Maddon moved out of hiding and headed towards the wagon. He pulled only sufficient branches away to get to it. He soon found the loose floorboard. As he lifted it, a tingle of excitement nipped at his gut to find it a false bottom.

What his gaze found, nestled in the cavity beneath it, were long parcels wrapped in greasepaper. Grim-faced he unwrapped one. It was the latest Winchester repeater. Incredulous, he counted a further nine, similarly protected.

Though tingling with excitement at the discovery, Maddon's brow furrowed. And the immediate thought that came to him didn't surprise him. Why? And why were they hidden — here?

He re-wrapped the gun; meticulously ensured things were as he had found them. Now he had to get back to Wallis. There was a great deal going on in this valley that needed answers. And now, he considered, urgent ones. There had to be a sinister reason behind men hiding weapons.

★ ★ ★

It was almost midnight by the time he reached Clayton. The town was asleep. Only two bars were open: disgruntled barkeeps waiting for card games to finish.

Maddon climbed stiffly off the back of the tired bay and saw to it she had a stall, feed and dry bedding at the livery barn, despite the hostler's garrulous protests about waking him.

After he had fully worked the numbness out of his legs Maddon made his way up to the sheriff's office. Through the window he could see Marty Collins sat back in the swivel chair, eyes closed.

As he entered, Marty became alert, his grey, keen eyes narrowing questioningly when he saw him.

"Howdy, Frank!" Then a small smile twisted the deputy's wide lips. "Still ain't found a bed?"

Ignoring the dry humour Maddon dumped his Winchester against the far wall and dropped into the chair at the table in the near corner. "Howdy, Marty! Guess Wallis has gone home, eh?"

Marty rose from his chair, his look direct. He nodded.

"Couple of hours ago."

Then he moved into the small room off the rear of the office next to the cells. He came back with a mug of steaming coffee.

Maddon took it gratefully, muttering

his thanks. He took a long, much-needed drink.

Marty narrowed his eyes now and searched Maddon's big, obviously tired frame. "Guess you ain't heard," he began.

Maddon narrowed his tired stare and searched the deputy's craggy face. "Heard what?" he demanded.

"Hannibal Mosely's been shot dead," the deputy replied. "He named Holly as his killer before he died."

Shock numbed Maddon for a moment. His reply was a gut reaction, along with his anger. "That's got to be a damned lie," he grated. "On whose say so?"

"Ace Pedlar and Rafe Emmet — a hand at the Rowel," supplied Marty. "Said they found Hannibal dying on the trail to the Rowel from Clayton. They'd been working cows in the area. They'd been alerted by shots."

Maddon made a disparaging noise. "By God, who'd believe a gunslinging varmint like Ace Pedlar?"

"Rafe Emmet backed him up," offered Marty. "An' like it or not, now, Pedlar's to be boss of the Rowel. An' that carries a lot of clout in some parts of this valley."

Maddon could no way accept the charge levelled against Holly. "Ace Pedlar is a gut-low card-sharp an' gunslinger," he growled meanly. "This Rafe Emmet's got to be bought an' paid for. What's Wallis done about it?"

Marty shrugged. "He had to bring Holly in, of course, though he weren't happy about it." The deputy's grey, steady gaze met Maddon's now. "He's out back, Frank — in cell one, if you want to talk with him."

Maddon found a cold rage was building up in him. "God damn it, this ain't right, Marty," he breathed. "Holly had no reason to kill Mosely. Mosely admitted to me only yesterday mornin' the Rowel had been wrongly on the prod over the water Walt had said belonged to them. Damn it, Hannibal said he'd ride over to apologise to Holly soon as he felt fit enough. And I let Holly know that."

The deputy shrugged. "I guess that's how Wallis views it, an' me for that matter," he said, "but until we got somethin' better to go on . . ."

Maddon rubbed his jutted jaw irritably, his face drawn and tired. "I'd like a word with Holly, Marty," he said. "Could you open up?"

The deputy nodded. "Sure."

He took the keys out of one of the desk drawers and unlocked the door leading to the brick cells connected to the back of the office. Holly was already at the bars of his cell and he greeted Maddon with a grim smile.

"Heard you talkin'," he said.

Maddon studied his brother. Holly was still calm-faced — a mirror image of himself. "I gotta ask," he said. "Did you, Holly?"

Holly made a dismissive noise. "No way, Frank," he said. "I could have done it long ago if I'd have wanted to."

Maddon nodded, his cold rage calming a little. "Sure you could," he said. "An' I know a few things that'll have you out of here in no time, Holly. Bank on it."

Holly grinned now. "I kind of hoped for somethin' like that, Frank. I got a crop of hay to get in. Usually a big family occasion, though Nathan an' Mat are worked enough at the moment. It's a busy time of year."

Maddon nodded again. "It is, eh? Well, keep your pecker up. Things'll be movin' purty soon." He gave his brother a long, warm look. "Be seein' you, Holly."

He went back into the office. He stared at Marty. "Time does Wallis turn in?"

"Around eleven o'clock if it's quiet," offered the deputy. "An' he don't like to be disturbed after that, unless it's real urgent."

Maddon made a rumbling noise deep in his chest and looked grimly at

Marty. "What I have to say'll jerk him up straight, or my name ain't Frank Maddon," he growled.

* * *

Wallis Tavener's house was in darkness. Maddon rapped briskly on the white front door under the long verandah roof.

It was a few moments before a light appeared in the room to the left of the door, then a window slid open and Wallis poked a disgruntled, sleep-tousled head through it.

"Don't you sleep, Frank?" he complained. "An' if it's about Holly — damn it it'll have to wait until mornin'."

He was about to slide down the window again when Maddon said, "I've found the owlhoots' hideout, Wallis, an' I know that Ace Pedlar's linked with them for sure."

The window came open again quickly. Tavener's blue eyes were wide-open now. "The hell you do," he breathed. His pink face set eagerly. "Give me five minutes to dress, Frank. I'll meet you at the office."

★ ★ ★

Twenty minutes later, Maddon watched Wallis's eyes narrow as he told the tale. When he finished both Marty and Tavener were staring hard at him.

"Rifles?" Wallis breathed then.

"New Winchesters," Maddon confirmed.

Wallis raised his sandy brows, obviously puzzled by the news. "Why hide them away?"

Maddon shook his head. "Beats me, unless . . . " The thought came out of the blue and he hardly believed it himself as he spoke it aloud. "Gun-runnin'?"

Wallis's face formed a doubtful look. He scrubbed his chin thoughtfully. "Who to?" he pondered. "And why? An' for what?"

Maddon shook his head. "I truly don't know," he admitted. "It's just a thought. I guess that's about the only reason why people hide guns — they want to sell them illegally."

Tavener still shook his head disbelievingly. "Ain't nobody I can think of to sell them to, unless . . . " His blue eyes opened, as though he couldn't believe the idea that came to him. "Not the broncos in the mountains?" he speculated incredulously. He shook his head again in disbelief. "Naw, it's too damned crazy."

Maddon stared at the small sheriff. "The Apaches would sure pay well for somethin' like that," he studied, "judging by the weapon one was carryin' when I had that run-in. An old Sharps. All the other came at me with was a knife."

Tavener's face was very serious as he said thoughtfully, "We've got to view it as a strong possibility — the 'why' will have to wait."

Then Wallis seemed to come to a

decision. "If they are for the Apaches, then we've got to act fast, boys," he said urgently. "We've gotta take that wagon. New Winchesters in the hands of the broncos could raise hell in the valley and all the way to the border, too, and give the army a mighty big headache for a while. 'Tain't two years since Geronimo surrendered an' got sent to Florida. There's still a lot of hate simmerin' out there."

Maddon, meantime, was thinking hard as well. "Maybe we could do better than just gettin' the guns, Wallis," he said then. "What would you say to substituting the real guns for greasepaper-wrapped wooden ones, weighted with lead to make 'em feel right, risk them foolin' Pedlar and his gunsels? I reckon it would prove to be mighty interestin' when the broncos find they've been duped."

Tavener rubbed the sandy bristles on his jaw. "Think we could pull it?" he questioned dubiously. "I don't want to risk nothin'. It'll depend on when, and if, a trade is on. An' if we've got the time."

Maddon met the sheriff's sudden, bright-blue stare. Then the lawman's eyes narrowed and the decision came swiftly. "We'll go for it, Frank," Tavener said then. "It could solve a lot of problems very quickly if it works."

Now Wallis turned to Collins. "Hold the fort, Marty. If anythin' crops up, we'll be at the undertaker's."

* * *

Tobias Fern lived over his carpenter's shop; a small, consumptive-looking bachelor with wispy brown hair and a wizened face. But Maddon was impressed by the keen black eyes that studied Wallis Tavener now — though the man had just been aroused from his bed — through the yellow light of the hoisted oil-lamp he carried.

Fern drew suspenders over a thick, brown, woollen shirt. "Couldn't it wait 'til mornin', Wallis?" he grumbled. "It's past midnight."

Tavener shook a negative. "Special job, Toby," he said.

He wasted no time on preliminaries and went on immediately to explain what he wanted.

The carpenter's eyes widened as he spoke. When the sheriff had finished, Fern gasped, "Well, if that ain't the damnedest request I've ever had."

"Can you do it?" urged Tavener.

Fern shrugged. "Sure, no problem. When fer?"

"Sun up?"

Fern's wizened features screwed up. "Gosh-darnit, Wallis," he complained. "That's a mite soon, ain't it?"

"Nothin' fancy, Toby," coaxed Tavener. "Just the right weight an' shape, like I said — wrapped in greasepaper. Me an' Maddon here'll help where we can."

Fern shrugged again. "Guess you'd better come in."

He backed from the door into his

workshop. The floor was six inches deep in sweet-smelling wood shavings. Maddon had always liked the odour.

Coffins, some made, some half-finished, showed in the yellow gloom, too. Also window frames, pine tables and chairs, wardrobes. Tobias Fern, thought Maddon, kept himself a busy man.

Fern squinted at the two lawmen. "Ever used carpenter's tools before?"

Maddon nodded along with Wallis. In more domestic days, when he had the general store business and was married to Martha —

The pain hit Maddon, as it always did, and he swallowed on the lump that had grown in his throat so quickly.

Well, he'd made some pretty nice pieces for the parlour . . .

★ ★ ★

By sun up, the job was done. Maddon, being honest with himself, would not have bet money on it, but there they were, ten greasepaper-wrapped replicas of Winchester repeaters weighted with lead and feeling pretty authentic.

Wallis beamed at him in the mellow light of the newly risen sun. "Toby, get yourself the best there is at the Rangeman's Rest, on my account, and send the bill for the job to the county," he said gratefully. Then warned: "But not a hint about the night's work yet, until I give the say so. Have I your word on that?"

Tobias Fern nodded, his wizened face unenquiring. "Sure, if that's how you want it, Wallis," he agreed. "Now, you mind if I get myself a couple of hours' shut-eye?"

He gave Maddon the distinct impression he required himself and Wallis to leave right now, and blew out the oil-lamps lit during the night to give the most light.

Both he and Wallis hefted five replicas apiece, each bundle wrapped in sacking, and moved out of Toby's untidy, and Maddon now found, cobweb-hung workshop.

The town was quiet and they moved quickly through it to the office.

Wallis stared at Maddon now, his face pale and tired-looking. "How far is it to the rifle cache?"

Maddon raised dark brows. "A good half-day ride if you pushed it."

Tavener tightened his small, rubbery lips. "Then we'd best get to it," he said.

He turned to Marty Collins. "I'll need you to hold the fort," he warned. "If we're unreasonably long gone get Shaney Weelon to spell you a few hours."

Marty nodded his craggy head. "No sweat, Wallis," he said. "But, damn it, I'd like to be in on this," he complained.

Tavener nodded sympathetically. "I know, Marty," he said. "But my guess is you're goin' to get all the action you need if this little ruse bears fruit."

★ ★ ★

They reached the wagon-cache mid-afternoon. The sun was harsh, even in the high foothills, and Maddon was feeling the full weariness of having had only a few hours fitful sleep in three days.

Now they held back. From a good vantage point Maddon scanned the area around them with his hunting glass. As far as he could see, there was no movement.

"We'd best get to it, Wallis," he said studying the sheriff's pale, now fatigued-looking face."

Tavener nodded and they eased their mounts down the trail to where Maddon knew the rifles were hidden.

The rifles were still there and they found boxes of cartridges, too. They made the switch swiftly, leaving things almost as they found them. Safely secured on the pack pony they had used to carry the rifles, they made back into the hills again overlooking the cache.

"I'd like to hang around for as long

as it takes to see what happens," Tavener said. "After all, it's all part of policin'. The waitin'. An' I think we'll get some mighty brisk answers to our questions if what we suspect turns out to be true."

Maddon nodded his grim concurrence eagerly. "It could turn out to be mighty interestin' indeed, Wallis."

"We got vittles enough," Tavener pointed out.

Even as Wallis spoke, Maddon narrowed his eyes, which were scanning the hills around them. He saw Indian smoke — and from the direction where he knew the owlhoot camp was. He brought Tavener's attention to it immediately.

The small sheriff's keen gaze studied him after he had perused the smoke.

"What do you think, Frank?"

"Well, it ain't no usual campfire, that's for sure," he said as he watched regular puffs rising into the azure sky.

Without a word being spoken, Maddon dismounted with Wallis. They secured their mounts and hunkered down in the clumps of brush and pines sprinkled across the rocky knoll they were hidden on.

After several minutes, the smoke stopped. They had to wait another half an hour before the signals were answered. The return smoke came from deeper south in the mountain range. Maddon met Tavener's knowing gaze.

"Got to mean some sort of action, Frank," Wallis commented.

Maddon grunted. "I got to agree."

Both men found comfortable positions and ate from billy-cans of cold beef stew Sarah Wallace had provided, assisted down with slices of gritty bread and tepid water.

★ ★ ★

The following day the dawn sun hit a cold, goose-pimpled Maddon for the second time in three days.

Blanket over his sheepskin coat he tramped around their make-shift camp, working life into his stiff knees and numbed toes.

And it annoyed him to see it didn't seem to be bothering Tavener, still in his blanket looking up at him.

"I'm gettin' too old for this, you know, Wallis," he complained bitterly.

The small lawman chuckled, threw his blanket back, stood up and stretched his small, stocky frame and pulled out his silver case. As if in sympathy, he offered Maddon a stogie. "Never figured you as havin' led a sheltered life, Frank," he commented innocently. "Maybe pampered a mite?"

Maddon growled sourly and glared and struck a sulphur match on his corduroy trousers. He lit his stogie fiercely, then offered the match to Tavener.

"It's a damned bit early in the day for that sort of talk, ain't it, Wallis?" he grumbled. Scowling, he scrubbed the dark, day-old beard on his determined chin.

Tavener still held his smile, lit

his stogie, his eyes twinkling and looked at Maddon's tousled, dark hair and unhappy face, and blanket-covered hunched shoulders, but didn't comment. He remembered, warmly, his pa had always been as grumpy as a butt-bit bear first ten minutes after he woke up, but it surprised him slightly to find Frank could be like that.

"Think we could risk a small fire?" he said. "A cup of hot coffee would go down real good, just now."

Maddon shook his head gloomily. "Best not risk it, Wallis," he said. "I got a feelin' pricklin' up my backbone it ain't goin' to be too long before things start poppin'."

Tavener nodded, serious now. "You got it too, eh?"

In silence they rolled blankets and tidied camp, took the horses off their hobbles and long ropes and watered them. Then they sat and chewed on cold, cooked beef and drank, because of the cold night, now ice-cold water from their canteens.

* * *

Mid-morning found Maddon, the sun warming his back, in better humour and keenly surveying the trail he expected the owlhoots to come down. He wasn't disappointed. With them were ten lean, copper-coloured Apaches.

And Ace Pedlar.

7

THEY rode in two separate bunches, and as they converged, each party eyed the other warily. At the cache, Ace Pedlar rode boldly forward and placed himself in front of the hiding place.

Then the talk started and the jug was passed round. But Maddon observed Pedlar was prudent enough to give the Apaches just enough to loosen them up a little but no more than that.

The one appearing to be the leader of the broncos began haggling fiercely. But there seemed to be no payment being made.

After a bargain appeared to have been struck, Pedlar waved an authorititive arm at two of his owlhoots, who climbed down and pulled aside the fir branches. Soon the chief bronco had one of the greasepaper-wrapped replicas in his hands.

Maddon felt expectant excitement now gnawing at his gut. He turned to find Tavener looking at him. The small lawman was licking his lips, his own taut enthusiasm clear in his bright blue eyes.

The brave unwrapped the replica eagerly. Then his cry of amazement and distrust carried even as far as Maddon's hideout.

With a guttural shout he thrust the replica back at Pedlar and backed off his sturdy pinto, his attitude suddenly menacing.

Pedlar was turning the wooden gun round and round in his palm, his astonishment clear, even from Maddon's position.

Then he seemed to be trying to reason with the bronco, but already the two sides were backing off, taking up aggressive positions. Then the crack of a rifle echoed up to Maddon's hideout. He watched one of the owlhoots throw back with a cry and fall to the ground.

All hell broke loose then and Maddon felt tension steel his limbs as he watched the drama unfold before him.

Pedlar dropped the replica as though it was suddenly red-hot. He clawed for his Colt. The bronco who had been doing the parleying kicked his pinto forward, his tomahawk raised to strike the gunslinger.

Pedlar parried the blow with a long left arm against the brave's forearm. As he did so he brought his Colt across the front of his stomach. Flame belched from its bore.

The bronco yelled and peeled off. He was obviously hit. And it seemed to galvanise him immediately into accepting it was a no-win situation for the broncos. He began shouting now and circling his tomahawk above his head.

Instantly the broncos disengaged, turned and started melting into the trees and hills around, shrilling their defiance and anger.

And Maddon knew from experience,

the Apache wasn't a fool and had half-expected the break. They were too thin on the ground now for such bravado. And the odds were too stacked in the white man's favour, even though the weight of numbers was on the broncos' side. The fact remained, and the Apache knew, a tomahawk was no match for a repeating weapon in competent hands.

The firing petered out to sporadic shots, then died away completely. The owlhoots were now riding round, angry and disorganised and endeavouring to calm their mounts. And also to come to terms with their sudden, obviously unwelcome change of fortune.

One of their number lay dead, another was limp in the saddle, clearly hurt. Two broncos were lying still in the grass.

Pedlar was already rapping orders as he dismounted and clambered onto the wagon. One by one he threw out the fake rifles. His curses reached up to Maddon and echoed even further into the now hot, shimmering hills.

Then Tavener declared, "I reckon we should take them, Frank."

Hearing the opinion Maddon felt a sudden, unaccustomed uncertainty niggle into him. He stared at the small sheriff. "We're buckin' big odds, Wallis," he said sceptically. "There's six of them down there. All hardened gunsels."

Tavener nodded, as if agreeing but argued, "We got one big thing in our favour, Frank — surprise. The last people they'll expect to see at the moment is us." Wallis looked at him now, a boyish eagerness on his face. "Frank, we could have the business cleared up come nightfall."

Maddon remained unconvinced. And he felt it right to voice his wariness. "They're keyed up," he pointed out tautly. "They'd fire at their own shadow right now." But then he shrugged, not wanting to appear yellow. "Still, if you figure we should do it — " He set his jaw " — well, I ain't a man to back away, Wallis."

Tavener smiled and nodded as if he had anticipated the reply. "I appreciate your caution, Frank," he said. "But I have a feelin' about this."

Now committed, Maddon said, grudgingly, "How do you reckon we should play it?"

Tavener moistened his small, elastic lips now. "Well, we could work in closer while they're still wonderin' what hit them. Then, while I caution them they are to be taken into the custody of the law, it would help if you put a couple of shots where it will mostly impress them if they show signs of aggression."

Uneasily Maddon checked his guns. They were — he knew without looking, but it was just a cautious habit — in good order. The scheme sounded a bit edgy to him, but then, Wallis was an experienced man.

He watched Tavener secure the packpony — allowing it generous rope to graze freely behind the screen of brush — check his own armoury, then look enquiringly at him.

"Ready, Frank?"

Maddon nodded and climbed up onto the back of his bay. He'd heard way back that Tavener was a man who was willing to take more than calculated risks. Their very daring had made them successful, but this . . .

Then Maddon succumbed to his occasional habit of mentally talking to himself: Are you really getting old, boy? he demanded. Is the fire in your belly really gone out? He blinked and spat sourly and followed Wallis as he led out.

They threaded forward through the brush and pine, working ever closer to the gunsels. As they got nearer, the ground dipped deeply before it rose again, taking them out of view of the owlhoots.

When they emerged again, they were less than two hundred yards from the gunsels and hidden by a thick clump of brushwood.

Tavener whispered. "Get yourself a

good firing position, Frank. I'm movin' in. If any one of them thinks he could get lucky, you have my authorization to shoot the bastard down."

Maddon felt the piano-wire-taut keenness fill him as his senses wound up.

"Right with you, Wallis," he breathed. "For God's sake be careful."

He tied the bay and worked to a position that overlooked the owlhoots, who, he saw, were now beginning to calm down. Ace Pedlar was back in the saddle and rapping curt orders about them moving camp and starting afresh, adding:

"The idea of arming the 'paches to clear out the small ranchers is a damned dead duck now, for sure, boys."

"I allus reckoned it a crazy one right from off," growled one of the gunsels. "You can't trust those mangy curs!"

Listening to the talk, Maddon's eyes slitted. Learning the reason for the cached guns filled him with disgust. How gut-low can a man get? his thoughts raged. He stared, his brown eyes hard, at the mean-looking gunslinger.

Pedlar growled, hearing the gunsel's opinion. "Yeah? Well listen, Tollance, I ain't askin' you for opinions," he snorted irritably. Then he glowered at the owlhoots. "An' that aside, we got more immediate problems. Somebody knows about this cache, and somebody has got our guns and somebody could blow our set-up sky high and maybe somebody knows apart from you I killed Hannibal Mosely, too."

It was then Tavener showed himself on the edge of the clearing, his rifle lined up on Ace. "I've got your guns, Ace," he informed. "And, yeah, your set-up's blown. And it's damned obligin' of you to tell us you gunned down Hannibal." The small sheriff narrowed blue eyes and lifted his chin authorititively. "Now drop your weapons, boys, easy-like, and raise your hands. Your day is up."

For moments, silence suspended the bright morning. Then, after the initial shock that had clearly staggered the owlhoots, scorn crossed Pedlar's leathery features.

"You must have gone out of your mind, Tavener," he hissed meanly. "There's six of us. We got to be able to blow you to kingdom come almost before you know it." His face lit up as a new thought seemed to come to him. "And we can blame the 'paches for it, too."

Maddon felt his hard muscles tightening further. Deliberately, and without hesitation, he shot off Pedlar's tall brown stetson leaving the gunslinger bareheaded. His grey stare swivelled and glared madly at the source from which the shot had come.

"Don't get ideas," Maddon called from his cover.

Pedlar, his aquiline face twisted with rage, turned his gaze back to Tavener. The small sheriff was calm, seated positively in the saddle, his Winchester lined up on the owlhoot.

It was then Pedlar seemed to go berserk.

He ripped out his Colt and started blazing away, shouting at the same time, "Hit them, boys."

Maddon set to firing, ignoring the lead that was suddenly hiving round him like a swarm of angry bees. He saw one owlhoot drop, Pedlar twist and clutch his upper arm.

Wallis was now trying to turn his mount to escape, firing and reloading the rifle with one hand before he cried in pain, spun off his horse and hit the ground.

That seemed a signal for the owlhoots to turn horses and flee, much, it seemed, to Pedlar's chagrin. "Come back, damn you!" he roared after them. "We got them!"

When he realised he was appealing to temporarily deaf men, Pedlar dug spurs and urged his roan after them, his curses still ringing through the hills.

Maddon reared up, pounding bullets

after the fleeing gunsels until the Winchester was empty. Then there was silence, except for the faint crash of brush and thud of hooves detailing the owlhoots' now distant flight. Then, that, too, died away rapidly.

Grim-faced, Maddon turned and ran down to Wallis now, who was moaning with pain on the ground. Blood had already crimsoned his shirt and levis down the right side.

"Must be losing my touch, Frank," he complained, with a grin that was more a grimace, creasing his round, pale face. "Shot twice in three days? Damn it, I can't sustain those sort of odds. But I guess one good thing has come out it. Holly can get back to his hay crop. Pedlar has sure let the cat out of the bag regardin' Hannibal."

Maddon, as happy as Wallis about Ace Pedlar's admission clearing Holly, felt loath to point out his own reluctance to carry out the daring bid to take the gunsels proving right, which had resulted in Wallis's bad wound. Instead, he grunted,

"Let me have a look at the wound, Wallis."

It was high up in the fleshy part of the left shoulder. The exit wound was a large, ragged hole bleeding badly.

"Feels as though," Wallis gasped, "it's ricocheted off my shoulder-blade and blew out under the armpit." Maddon found Tavener's eyes were questioning him, as if seeking confirmation. "Right?"

Maddon met the lawman's blue, pain-filled gaze. "Seems that way." Then he said, though realising the small lawman possibly knew, "You're losing too much blood, Wallis."

Tavener nodded and waved weakly towards his horse. "In my saddle bags, Frank. You'll find bandages. Allus carry some, jest in case . . ."

Without comment Maddon left the lawman. Sure enough, a sizeable wad of clean cotton pads and wrappings.

When he returned, he found Wallis had somehow managed to peel off his shirt, and Maddon worked on the bloody wound patiently. When he had done, he stepped back, a stir of admiration in him. He hadn't done too bad a job, he reckoned. He had slowed down the bleeding considerably.

"Figure you can ride, Wallis?" he said.

Tavener studied him for a moment. "Well, there's only one way to find out, Frank," he grunted. "Hand me up."

Maddon heaved the game little sheriff to his feet as gently as he could. Tavener gasped with pain once, that was all, but the colour had drained from his round face completely now, leaving it ashen.

★ ★ ★

Halfway down the trail to Clayton, both men fighting the heat and the fatigue it caused, Wallis sagged in the saddle, his face drawn, the skin having the appearance of putty. His pain-filled stare caught Maddon's concerned gaze.

"I got to rest, Frank," he said huskily.

Maddon knew the small sheriff was still losing blood — not much, but enough. "We should git on, Wallis," he urged. "You need Doc Fredricks' attentions."

"I know," Tavener admitted. "But I just can't seem to hold myself up, Frank."

The small sheriff swayed again. It took what seemed a supreme effort of will to keep himself in the saddle. He unhitched his canteen of water and drank long and thankfully.

"Maybe you should press on alone to Clayton, Frank," he suggested. "Send somebody back up the trail with a buckboard for me."

Maddon growled at the proposal. "What kind of a man do you think I am, Wallis?" he demanded, feeling hurt.

Tavener's still bright blue stare met his own. "A practical one, is my guess," he said. He fought for breath for a moment. "What we gonna lose, anyway? Maybe two hours? I figure it'd do me more good to lie still, 'stead of bouncin' around on a horse."

Maddon studied the stocky sheriff and he had to agree: yes, it was an eminently practical suggestion. It just stuck in his craw, though, to admit defeat on anything. There must be a way to take Wallis with him.

"I can't do it, Wallis," he said firmly. Then, "Maybe if you sat up here with me, I could hold you on."

A faint, grateful smile spread Wallis's small lips. "Thanks, Frank," he muttered, "but it ain't on. I'm losing too much blood, jogging around." His eyes pleaded now. "Help me off and prop me up under that cottonwood over there. I'll be all right. Bet on it."

Maddon felt gut-low about the whole business. "Damn it, Wallis," he protested. "It ain't my way . . ."

Tavener nodded patiently. "I know it," he said weakly. "But you've got to admit, it makes sense. And, damn it, anyway, now I'm through talkin' — I'm tellin' you to do it!"

The effort Tavener put into the demand, left him coughing painfully. But Maddon was glad to see no blood came from the mouth.

Maddon finally decided that Wallis's idea was a better bet all round, though, God knew, it hurt to have to submit to it.

He sighed and climbed down. "You win, Wallis."

Tavener shook his head slowly. "No — you do, Frank. I don't call many men 'friend', but you're one I'm proud to."

Maddon reached for the game sheriff. "Well, I got a damned poor way of returning your regard," he grumbled.

Tavener's laugh came weakly before he started to keel over. Anxiously, Maddon stepped forward and took the full weight of the heavy sheriff in his sinewy arms as he slid out of his saddle.

"Sorry, Frank," Tavener grunted.

"But I feel so light. I feel as though I'm floatin'." He passed out completely then.

★ ★ ★

Maddon had got Tavener under the cottonwood when the three Apaches broke cover. He stared disbelievingly as they took Wallis's horse and the pack-pony, both ground-hitched on the trail. Then they went howling off into the blue hills with their prize almost before he could spit.

Rampant rage rushed through him as he saw the Winchesters and ammunition disappearing into the hills, towed by a near-naked savage. He raced for his Winchester, pouched in the holster on the back of his bay. It had been sheer mechanical habit that he had led the bay to the cottonwood, before carrying Wallis to its shade.

He sent angry shots after the whooping braves.

Then silence. He stood quivering, his

rage still red-hot. He stared after the impudent broncos before throwing his stetson to the ground in utter disgust and blueing the air with curses. But, even more grave, he realised, was the fact the Apaches now had the guns he and Wallis had taken such pains to avoid them receiving.

Maybe they didn't know what they had stolen. Maybe it had just been an opportunist, cheeky raid to gain a pack pony and a good quality horse while a white man had been off guard . . . He knew they could be that arrogant.

Maddon growled and spat furiously at being caught so easily.

Impatiently, he turned to Tavener. One thing was for sure — he couldn't leave Wallis here now. And God knew what would happen when the broncos came to a standstill and found what they had plundered.

Wallis was now conscious again and Maddon quickly explained what had happened.

Tavener growled, his blue eyes

narrowing. "Damn and blast it," he raged weakly. "Seems like our luck's plumb played out at the moment, Frank."

Then, like a man used to meeting adversity head on, he smiled through his pain, "Guess we'll have to double up after all," he grunted. "At the moment, we ain't a deal runnin' for us, have we?"

Maddon scowled, still feeling as though his rage was spur-raked raw now at being so outdone by the renagade Apaches.

"That's a damned understatement, Wallis, if I ever heard one," he said irately. He leaned forward then and extended a lean, but sinew-corded arm. "Give me your hand."

The effort of getting into the saddle left Tavener sagging heavily against Maddon's broad, muscular chest as he got up behind him. The afternoon sun was strong on them both and not helping.

After a watchful scan of the hills

around them, Maddon urged the bay towards the softer meadowlands of the Wassala Valley and Clayton. He wondered why the hell he'd got himself into this situation. He could have been haymaking at Holly's place. He scowled momentarily as the thought came to him.

But he knew damn well, as Wallis had earlier said: basically, he was a lawman at heart. And nothing would alter that . . .

8

DOC FREDRICKS worked swiftly on Wallis's unconscious body. Fifteen minutes later he told Maddon, and Tavener's family visiting with him, the plucky little sheriff had a fighting chance, but he would be a sick man for some time to come.

With the information ringing in his ears, Maddon walked up the oil-lamp-lit street to the office. From the swivel chair, Marty Collins stared at him — clearly expecting news about the sheriffs condition. The deputy knew the story of the guns. Maddon had told him earlier, after he'd stabled his horse and while they had waited for Doc Fredricks to deal with Wallis.

"How is he, Frank?"

Maddon tightened his thin lips. "Well, he ain't good, Marty," he said.

"That's for damned sure."

Marty's look was questioning now. "Seems like the only good thing to come out of this business so far was gettin' Holly cleared of gunnin' down Hannibal." The deputy narrowed his gaze. "Think Wallis was right goin' after Pedlar's gunsels like he did?"

"Guess he figured it was the thing to do."

Maddon wanted to turn the subject. He wasn't going to criticize Wallis now. It would have been a master stroke if they had pulled it off. They hadn't banked on Pedlar going crazy. Who would?

"We've got to do our damnedest to try and get those rifles back, Marty," he said, to swing the conversation, "and pull Ace Pedlar and his gunhawks in."

Marty nodded his agreement, blinking his grey eyes. "Yeah. I guess that's got to be priority." He compressed his lips, grimly. "But it's a tall one."

Maddon studied the well-built, dark, craggy deputy lounged in the chair.

"Wallis said it would be none too difficult to raise a posse here," he explored. "That so?"

Marty nodded an affirmative. "We had a deal of trouble with 'paches when Geronimo was on the prod two, three years ago, before Crook caught up with the murderin' devil in Mexico," he said. "There were times when we raised posses of as many as thirty men."

Maddon felt heartened by the news. "Well, do you think they will mind bein' pulled out of their beds this time? 'paches roaming the countryside with the latest Winchesters ain't a prospect to relish. And the sooner that varmint, Ace Pedlar, is brought to book the better."

Marty came to his feet with a grunt. "There's only one way to find out, Frank," he said, "an' that's for me to go an' ask."

He narrowed his eyes and looked at the tall, grim, raw-boned man before him. A man powdered with dust and sweat-salt. A man stained with Wallis's blood. A man haggard through lack of sleep. And with two days growth of black beard on his chin.

"Why don't you washdown and get a couple of hours' shut-eye, Frank, while I get to organizing things?"

Maddon had a nagging gut-feeling he should be getting on with the urgent business the events of the day had thrown up, feeling partly responsible for them, but then, Marty was an experienced peace officer and knew the town, and its people, better than he did.

He sighed heavily. "Well, I wouldn't say no to that, Marty," he accepted. "An' thanks."

Marty smiled and waved a dismissive hand. "Hell, 'tain't nothin'," he said. "I get a mite sick of sittin' on my ass. After midnight Saturday night, when the boys have gone back to punchin' cows, this ain't the most interestin' of jobs, I can tell you."

★ ★ ★

As Marty left the office to gather the posse, Maddon considered sleep, his mind reviewing what had passed since entering town, Wallis Tavener slumped unconscious in his arms.

He had told Holly of Ace Pedlar's unguarded and unsolicited confession in the hills as soon as he had hit town. And had immediately released his brother with Wallis's agreement, leaving the cell block now empty.

Holly had promptly ridden home to prepare to defend what was his against a possible Apache attack. Maddon wanted like hell to join him, but his first duty, he knew, was here.

Now, too tired to wash up, Maddon slumped onto one of the cell beds and dropped into a deep sleep.

It was coming light when Marty shook him awake. Feeling sour, the taste in his mouth akin to a well-used buffalo wallow, Maddon protested, "Damn it, it can't be that time. I've just got to sleep."

Sat on the bunk edge he looked

mournfully up at the deputy. "Why the hell did I sign on for this, Marty?" he grumbled unreasonably. "Damn it, I'm getting too old for it."

Marty stuck a cup of steaming coffee under his nose. "Try that, Frank," he said. Maddon didn't see the smirk on the deputy's face. He was too busy feeling sorry for himself.

Then Maddon said, "How about the posse?"

"Twenty-two men have agreed," the deputy supplied. "We meet outside the office half an hour after sun up."

Grateful for that piece of news Maddon drank thankfully, coughing and gasping for breath as the last mouthful went down the wrong way sending him grumpy again. "Damn it," he groused. "Does everything allus have to happen to me?"

He sat on the cell bed for a few moments longer, head in hands and scrubbing his beard and attempting to resolve he wouldn't always wake up as bad-tempered as a burr-bothered burro. Then he rose. "Where can I wash up, Marty? Didn't get round to it last night."

"Water next door in the little room. Soap an' towels there, too. You'll find my shavin' gear in there. You're welcome to use it."

Maddon 'humphed' his thanks and drew off his shirt and vest and began to scrub.

Fifteen minutes later he was cleaner and feeling a whole lot better. He walked down to Sarah Wallace's Eatery and found — even at this early hour, the sun not yet risen — the homely-looking woman was busy lighting the cook-stove fires and had coffee simmering on the pot-bellied stove top in the eating area.

"Mornin', ma'am," he said. "Ham an' eggs when you're ready."

"Morning, Mr Maddon. A fair day."

Maddon nodded and lit his pipe. "Truly is, ma'am," and waited for his breakfast.

Half an hour later he was outside in

the street again stepping towards the office, picking his teeth and belching his satisfaction and staring at the sun starting to rose the tops of the false-fronts lining the street. He felt more like a human being again.

It was then the rider came thundering down the main street, straight up to the sheriff's office.

Marty was already out of the office catching the rider as he fell out of the saddle. Maddon sprinted to his side.

"'paches," the man was gasping haltingly, his face haggard with pain. "Last night . . . Burnt us out . . . Made off towards the Rowel . . . " The man's hand trembled up. "Damn it, I thought we'd seen the last of them, Marty."

It was then Maddon saw the hole in the man's back where the bullet that had hit him in the chest had exited and wondered how he had kept astride his horse. As his words died from his lips the man flopped unconscious. It was clear to Maddon the man was breathing his last.

He looked questioningly at Marty. "Who is he?"

"Saul Jepson," Marty delivered. "Has a small-holding six miles out of town on the Shady Creek trail." Now the deputy looked up at Maddon, his lived-in face serious. "Appears as though the broncos are heading for the Rowel to give Ace Pedlar a lesson after the business with the guns, if what Saul says is good information."

Maddon nodded bleakly. "I'm inclined to agree."

Pedlar and his gunsels, Maddon wasn't worried about. The Apache could do as they damned well liked with them — if they could take the owlhoots, that is. That hard-bitten crew would give a good account of themselves, he knew, though it galled him to admit it to himself. He had no time for murdering rubbish like them.

But he guessed there were sound, honest rangemen that rode for the Rowel, too. Hannibal Mosely had proved, though a vindictive man, to be also an honourable one.

Maddon blinked at the deputy. "It's got urgent now, Marty," he grunted. "But maybe we can kill two birds with one stone here."

Marty stared at him, his grey eyes now hard steel. "We sure as hell are goin' to have to try, Frank," he said. "And I'm comin' with you this time."

★ ★ ★

Half an hour later Maddon cast his tawny gaze over the posse assembled before the office.

They were a grim-faced bunch of men sat astride their mounts, warming themselves in the early morning sun. Some wore long dust coats, others range gear, others broadcloth suits and Derby hats. But all had one thing in common: the business-like rifles which were held as though they knew full-well how to use them; and Colts of varying ages — from Walkers to the latest Peacemaker — tucked into waistbands, or pouched in holsters.

Even Doc Fredricks joined them at the last minute, a big Sharps rifle stuffed in the boot near his right thigh. He had a Remington .44 tucked into a fancy holster, too.

Also, there were pack mules loaded with food, medical accessories, ammunition and water. Maddon was impressed. Definitely, as Marty had assured him, this wasn't the first posse these men had served on.

They rode out an hour after sun up, pushing northwards towards the Rowel.

Almost as soon as they had cleared the outskirts of the town, Maddon saw the thin pillar of smoke rising above the undulating grasslands of the Wassala Valley.

"Got to be Saul Jepson's place," Marty informed, riding his skittish little pinto beside him. His face was drawn and sober. "God knows what we'll find."

Twenty minutes later they rode up

to the smouldering ruins of what, reckoned Maddon, had been a tidy little farmhouse. But the other things they found caused Maddon to fight to keep his breakfast.

The woman was spreadeagled over a mound of earth. It didn't take any figuring out she had been raped repeatedly before she had been shot in the vagina and filled with arrows and her mouth stuffed with dirt.

The boy, the ancient Sharps near him — Maddon judged him to be fifteen, around Nathan's age — had had his throat slit and his eyes gouged out, his testicles removed.

The two girls . . . well . . . the devil's fires burnt in Maddon's eyes to see what they had done to them.

Half an hour later Doc Fredricks read the twenty-third Psalm over the mounds of earth and Maddon could not quell the feeling of guilt roiling in him. If he had tried harder to talk Wallis out of attempting to take the owlhoots on and concentrate on getting the rifles and ammunition back to Clayton, maybe the Jepsons would still have been a happy, settled family going about their daily chores right now.

Marty stirred restlessly in the saddle beside him as they now urgently rode off towards the Rowel, his grey eyes studying him intently. The deputy said, "You're blamin' yourself for losing the rifles, ain't you?"

Maddon nodded, anger still flaming within him. "To put it mildly. Yes."

"Well, Wallis thought it was right at the time," the deputy observed. "I figure I would have gone along with him. Wallis is rarely wrong with his hunches."

"I could have argued harder against," Maddon bit out. "To tell you truly, Marty, I didn't go along with the idea."

Marty pursed his grim, generous lips. "You could have argued, I guess," he agreed. "But once Wallis has reached a decision there was no way I know that would turn him. And I've known him six years."

Maddon levelled his gaze and looked forward, staring at the vast green valley spreading before him to the blue mountains to the north.

Maddon nodded. "It'll fade with time, I reckon," he said tiredly. "All things do that. But it never stops you rearin' up in bed at times, the sweat rollin' off you, the sight of those two girls . . ."

Marty's response was harsh and dry. "Yeah," he said bleakly. "That's the damned truth of it, I guess."

The posse had lapsed into bitter silence, too. Obviously they were outraged by the findings at the Jepson homestead. Maddon reckoned it wasn't the first tortured and abused homestead they had attended. But, despite that, he knew, you never quite got used to it.

Mid-afternoon they saw the smoke rising in the still air — a black, thick column stark against the blue vault.

Grim, knowledgeable looks passed

between the posse. Maddon knew it had to be the Rowel. He knew the trail, and knew they were no more than an hour's ride from the ranch.

He could sense the keening edge of urgency running through the posse, who had been slumped in the saddle, grudgingly bearing the onslaught of the fiery orb above them as noon had neared and passed. Even frequent pauses for water for men and horses hadn't helped much. And the salt beef they were chewing only added to their problems.

But, like a flock of migrating birds, they started to move forward briskly and in unison, though no voice had urged them to canter.

Half an hour later they could hear the crisp cracks of rifle fire. Brisk exchanges interspersed with snapping, desultory shooting.

The posse fanned out into a line and crested the rise overlooking the Rowel — a big spread crouched below the foothills rising to the mountains.

Two barns were ablaze but the main ranchhouse was intact and fierce gunfire was issuing from the gun slits built into it. Maddon guessed this was not the first attack the Rowel had withstood.

The Apaches were dismounted, their wiry mounts — screened from the ranch in a rill some stream, now dry, had dug out in years gone by — held by three boys, secure in good cover.

Maddon met Marty's narrow stare. "They've run off the Rowel remuda," he said tersely. "They allus keep the working horses in that corral down by the river."

Maddon nodded. He remembered seeing that when he and Wallis had visited. The big barn down there was a raging conflagration. Timothy hay did tend to burn fast and bright, he thought grimly.

Maddon took out his hunting glass. He picked out twelve braves, ten with Winchesters . . .

He looked grimly at the posse all lined up and stern-visaged, staring at

Maddon and Marty, as if wanting some guidance as to how they could best tackle the situation.

"I reckon we should go straight in," Maddon said, authority in his voice. "Six men try and cut the broncos off from their horses. It'll be close run, but off-hand, I can't think of any better way."

Then a warning whoop came from one of the boys holding the horses. Immediately, the broncos were searching their surroundings with fierce eyes sizing up the situation, and Maddon cursed. They had been so eager to get at the murdering heathen, they'd sat on the skyline like crows on telegraph wire waiting to be seen.

The broncos were now running, crouched low to the ground, straight for their mounts.

Firing welled up from the ranch-house. The range the Apaches had kept to was close enough for long-range fire, but, in an emergency like this, far enough away to be soon out of range.

Maddon didn't see one bronco drop.

Maddon thought, with reluctant admiration, they were no fools at this deadly game.

With a shout he put the bay into a gallop. The posse moved in behind him and the race was on.

Maddon knew their horses were tired and couldn't sustain a prolonged run. But, if only for the Jepson family, by God, they had to try!

He soon discovered the Apaches could run almost as fast as a horse in a spurt and they were on their stocky horses before the posse had got into effective rifle range. Desperate frustration was already beginning to build up in Maddon.

He urged the bay into further efforts. But once the broncos had got their horses into stride they were already perceptibly pulling away from the posse.

Grim-faced now, Maddon reined his horse to a halt, holding up his hand to signal the posse to do likewise.

"It's no good, men," he grated, his throat dry. "We'll kill our horses trying to catch them. I reckon we get back to the Rowel and see if there's any work for Doc Fredricks to do. We'll maybe rate a steak as well. And there's a gent I very much want to see maybe holed up there, too."

One of the posse nearby grunted. "Guess you've said it all, Maddon. But we sure as hell got to try our best to get them damned 'paches before they make it out of the mountains."

Marty Collins said, "I reckon when they get out of the valley they'll head south for Mexico rampaging and looting their way across the territory like they allus used to. Somebody ought to ride back to Clayton and telegraph the army they're comin', now we know the situation. And they're broncos. They ain't likely to be hampered with wives and children."

★ ★ ★

The posse dealt with the decision about the man to return to Clayton. The man they chose, it was decided, would ride back when he had eaten and rested his horse a spell.

The rangemen at the Rowel greeted them warmly and the cook soon had steaks sizzling on the skillet. Two rangehands had suffered gunshot wounds; one serious. Doc Fredricks got to work straightaway.

A man who, Maddon learned from Marty, was the Rowel straw boss, name of Brad Mullins, informed them that Ace Pedlar had rode in yesterday evening. Told them to stay close to the ranch and expect Apache trouble.

Brad Mullins' grey eyes queried Marty and Maddon. "Now, how the hell did he know that?" he said.

Maddon tightened his dust-rimed lips. "It's a long story," he said. Then, more eagerly: "Where is he, Mullins?"

"Why, he lit out with a bunch o' hombres I ain't seen afore," offered Brad. "Said he had business. The men backin' him looked real hardcases to me. And one seemed to be hurt bad."

Mullins turned to Marty now, ignoring Maddon. "I ain't never taken to that Pedlar hombre," he grumbled. "Ever since Walt brung him here."

Mullins narrowed his keen eyes. "He has a mean streak. An' I don't cotton to him bein' boss now Walt an' Mr Mosely are dead, though, o' course, he won't be." The straw boss wagged his head. "Even so I don't fancy bein' bossed by the syndicate Mr Mosely told me about, who are supposed to have shares in the place, either."

Maddon's ears snapped up the information.

Marty said, "You mean Ace Pedlar ain't in line for the ranch?"

The straw boss's eyes widened. "Mr Mosely had no time for that hombre," he growled. "If it didn't go to Walt — he said the syndicate would buy it out and each man would have a cut of the profit. Now, that was damned wide of Hannibal, weren't it?"

Mullins turned, leather-faced and resentful, to Maddon now. Frank met his steely stare. "Even so, you did us no favours killin' Walt, mister," he growled. "An' with that damned brother o' yourn killin' Mr Mosely. Goshdarnit, that was the last straw. I don't know how you got the gall to come ridin' in here like this showin' your tin badge."

"Ace Pedlar kilt Hannibal, Brad," Marty supplied evenly. "Holly had nothin' to do with it."

Brad Mullins looked hard at the deputy, shock clear on his face. "The hell you say? Who told you that?"

"Pedlar did. Shot his mouth off when he thought he wasn't bein' heard. I guess he figured the ranch would come to him. Must have come as a surprise when he found it didn't."

Mullins screwed his eyes up and looked disbelievingly at the deputy. "Rafe Emmet swore to God Mr Mosely named Holly Maddon," he said incredulously.

"He weren't tellin' the truth," Maddon cut in. "Where is he?"

"He rode out with Pedlar."

"When did he join the Rowel bunkhouse?" Maddon pursued.

"Soon after Walt brought Ace in."

Maddon eyed Marty. It seemed to Maddon the statement cleared away any last doubts there may have been about Holly's innocence. It was pretty clear to a lawman's mind that the whole thing had been a set-up and that Rafe Emmet was Pedlar's man.

Maddon kept his stare on Marty. "We've got to run this varmint down," he said grimly. "And I think I know where he's run to earth. And I think he don't know I know. And maybe he thinks the 'paches don't know, either. And I think he's mistaken there, too."

The deputy blinked. "That's a mouthful, Frank." He smiled. Then he went serious again. "I figure those broncos will want Pedlar's blood before they quit Wassala Valley," he said, joining with Maddon's line of thought.

"Do you reckon our luck's about to change?"

Maddon jutted his grim, black-stubbled jaw. "It's due to, by God," he growled resentfully. "I want that bastard, Pedlar — if only for Wallis's sake, Marty."

The craggy deputy looked owlishly at him. "Well, I'll drink to that, Frank."

9

IT was three hours after dark. Upright and determined the posse was heading south to the owlhoot hideaway Maddon had found in the mountains.

Maddon had no serious doubts about his hunch that they would find the gunsels there, and, eight to one, the broncos. There were scores to settle before the Apaches decided on going anywhere was his bet . . .

Marty rode quietly beside him. A big, yellow moon towered above them making the trail clear as day and easy to travel.

Then Marty said, "I was brung up in Texas. Know what they call a moon like that there, Frank?"

Maddon shook his head, interested.

"A Comanche moon. Before the red devils were herded into reservations they would get close to settlements, hole up until the moon was full, then strike and run north again to count their scalps and spoils, leavin' death and destruction behind them."

Maddon watched the deputy's eyes narrowing as if terrible memories were coming back. "You think the 'pache mean, Frank?" he said quietly. "I've seen some of those things the Comanches did. Honest to God . . ."

The deputy shook his head and looked sad-eyed at him. And Maddon wondered if Marty had suffered a family loss through Comanches.

Maddon nodded. "I've heard about them heathens, though I ain't had much experience of them. 'paches with me, mostly, an' Southern Cheyenne. Did have a few brushes with the Kiowa. Related to the Comanche, ain't they?"

Marty nodded. "Sort of, I heard."

After that the talk petered out. Both men lapsed into a brooding, watchful silence.

They left the valley and started into

the foothills. By the time the moon dipped below the white tips of the mountains ahead they were at the head of the tree-choked ravine Maddon had first negotiated when he had trailed the owlhoots to their hideout.

The first pearl signs of false dawn were showing when Maddon ordered the posse to halt and dismount and feed themselves. They were now on the slope rising to the flat clearing Maddon knew the gunsels' hideout was on.

While they ate Maddon said to the posse generally, "The owlhoot camp is above. I figure we should get in as close as we can and encircle it. They're sure to have men posted, so we'll have to be real quiet about this one — "

The bark of rifles interrupted anything else he had to say. It was a savage calamity of noise snarling into the mountain vastness, its echoes cannoning off the eternal peaks receding to lonely distances.

Immediately, Maddon thought: Apaches. Mild surprise came to him.

If they were, his hunch had hit plumb centre.

Then he could hear the shouts of the owlhoots. Maddon sifted out Pedlar's voice, rapping calm, clear orders. The man was no yellow-belly, he had to grudgingly admit that.

Then the firing rose to even more fierce heights.

Marty, his eyes gleaming with excitement as he looked at Maddon, growled, "It's goin' to be some humdinger up there."

Maddon nodded, feeling his own exhilaration unleashing itself. "We got to surprise the 'paches, Marty, an' catch us some varmints as well. We got to bank on them bein' so busy up there they ain't time to look for us. I guess even 'paches, bent on vengeance, can get a little careless."

He scanned the tree-filled slope rising above them. He knew, by the detailed scan of the area he'd done when he had first found the hideout, the trail up to the owlhoots' camp went off east first before swinging west again, back to the camp. It was maybe a three mile detour — but the only hidden way up there for a horse.

A plan formed swiftly in his mind. He stared at Marty. "I figure three men to take the horses up the trail to the camp — I'll point out the path — and the rest of us filtering in on foot — so many men below, so many men above. Then flush out that scum."

"Have the men below as a sort of catch-net an' set up a crossfire?" Marty added, quick to pick up Maddon's trend of thought.

Maddon nodded, his eyes now bright with the thought of the action to come.

"We'll have to be real careful," the deputy counselled. "The 'pache aren't easy men to fool."

Maddon nodded grimly. "I know it."

When Maddon put the plan to the posse, there was general agreement that it was the best available to them.

Maddon elected to lead the party who were to gain the high ground, while Marty took the rest straight up the side of the mountain.

Maddon looked round the serious-faced men now, their breaths condensing in the cold air, hunched against the dawn chill. Most were checking hardware, with the panache of men who knew all about guns and the use of them. It heartened Maddon to see it.

The sun's rays were now painting strawberry pink on the white tips of the mountains behind them, but the ravine below looked blue-cold and wreathed with mist.

Tight-lipped, Maddon scanned the pale, taut men surrounding him.

"Right, men," he said quietly. "Let's get to it and good luck."

Maddon set off at a loping run heading west and describing a wide arc up through the close-growing pines.

And all the time they were doing it, the sound of guns above ripped to shreds the usual calm solitude of the peaks.

It suited Maddon. Such intense fire had a wonderful way of concentrating the mind on survival and the business at hand, and not on a possible ambush.

It was getting steep now and the laboured breathing of the men behind him came to him plainly. Maddon found his own lungs were now pumping fast to take in the extra oxygen they were needing.

It was then he saw them, and he stopped and crouched low. There they were in a small, tree-shaded clearing. Two blanket-wrapped, shivering Apache boys with the Indian horses. He moistened his lips. It was sent from heaven.

The boys were listening eagerly to the fighting and oblivious to anything else around them.

"Take them alive," he whispered to the men behind him. "I ain't partial to killin' colts."

"Sure you've heard it said, Maddon,"

a hard-eyed man grunted beside him. "Nits make lice . . . ?"

Maddon stuck out his chin. "Not if we can avoid it," he hissed tersely. "Keep it quiet. No shootin'."

He looked cold-eyed at the men around him. Though some appeared in doubt, they nodded.

They moved in fast. The boys had no chance. While they were trussed they were kicking and biting like mountain cats at the rough hands over their mouths, until they were gagged with their own headbands.

Let loose, the nervous, wiry horses scattered into the trees, down the slope, running free.

Maddon was relieved to see them running away from the fracas roaring death some distance to the east of them now. That put the Apaches on foot. But even on foot, they were still a daunting prospect. Then the thought hit him: there were still the owlhoots' horses, though. If they got to them . . .

Then Maddon brought himself up dead. Damn it! He was thinking himself more trouble than he already had!

He looked round the posse again and waved the Winchester in his hand for them to move forward again.

Twenty minutes later they knew they were above the broncos. They could catch glimpses of them now, flitting through the trees like shadows, changing position frequently.

Shooting was sounding from firing points all around the cabin in the clearing. The owlhoots' horses were rope-corralled against a flat up-thrust of rock in the centre of the clearing to the west of the cabin. Two were dead, another was threshing on its side. Victims of ricochets, he wondered speculatively? He couldn't imagine Apaches shooting good horseflesh without some very urgent reason.

Maddon cast a tawny stare at the men with him. "This is it, men," he muttered grimly. "Pick your target and make it as sure as you can. Fire when the shooting rises to a height to mask it. Then, I guess, it'll take them a little while to realise they are boxed in."

Grim-faced the posse dispersed. Each man found his cover and Maddon crouched himself behind the bole of a tall pine.

The sun's rays were now beginning to filter down through the canopy, warming them.

Then Maddon found his first target. His man came bellying across the pine needles to a rock poking out of the hillside. The bronco snaked up behind it and pressed flat-bellied on it, pushing his new Winchester through a cleft in the rock towards the cabin. He commenced aiming and firing with deliberate intent.

Maddon drew his bead on the head of the bronco, plumb centre of the black hair patch in the middle of the Indian's red headband. Momentarily, in his mind's eye, he saw the two girls at the Jepson place and he had no qualms about shooting a man from behind. Almost as soon as he had squeezed off, the bronco slumped, his smashed, bloodied head flattened into the rock. He didn't move again.

Narrow-eyed, Maddon stared around him, seeking a new target now, his hunting spirit welling up with the first drawn blood.

Yes. He saw his next man moving up a depression in the hillside. And it could be a way to the cabin, his practised eye observed. The Apache was certainly giving it a lot of attention.

He waited for a rise in the shooting. When it came, it came from where Marty's party must be. Now the surprise must surely be exploded.

It didn't deter him, though. He squeezed off. His next Apache shouted and spun round, his hands pressed to his gut, his Winchester falling to pine needles.

Maddon levered another shell into the breech and sent more lead hammering into the falling Apache. This time the bronco flung back, thumping into the tree bole behind him before spinning round and falling. He rolled down the incline to finish up draped against the base of a tall pine.

Bronco whoops started now, behind him. Maddon was just in time to stick out his Winchester and trip the redman as he came crashing out of the brush, across the hill, through the trees, past him. He was obviously making for the horses.

Fight fever now blood-red in him, Maddon rose and ran to the bronco. The Apache was rolling onto his back now, his Winchester coming up to deal death, his eyes mirrors of hellish hate.

Maddon fired from the hip, his lead smashing into the bronco's chest. He felt the Indian's own lead burning his cheek as he did so. His second shot hit over the bronco's heart. Blood came gushing from his mouth. But still he had fight.

He was trying to lever another shell into the breach when Maddon thrashed the rifle from his grasp with the butt of his own piece. Then the bronco flopped back, quivered, his back arched, then relaxed and his sightless eyes were staring at the grey squirrel oddly perched, studying him from the canopy.

Then Maddon realised the firing was petering out, to become desultory. Slowly it faded to a time-suspended silence which seemed unnatural after the calamity of noise.

Maddon listened intently for moments. The tree-clad slope and clearing below, with the owlhoot cabin at its centre, was now, suddenly, funeral-quiet.

After breath-baited minutes Marty called from below, "You okay, Frank?"

It was met with a crash of guns from the cabin but from nowhere else. Either the broncos were dead, or those who remained had faded into the trees and left, finding the cost too great.

Maddon waited for the barrage to peter out before bawling,

"Pedlar! You and your men are surrounded. There is a posse of twenty-two men here who'll have no qualms about gunnin' you down if need be. I suggest you throw out your guns and surrender peaceable."

Silence followed for moments, before Pedlar snorted, "Go to hell!"

Maddon narrowed his eyes. "I repeat. You men in the cabin, don't listen to Pedlar, whatever he says. As near as I know, what you've done so far has caused only a nuisance and maybe rates a year in the territory prison. But Pedlar'll hang for the killin' of Hannibal Mosely. If you stay in there, so help me, we'll smoke you out if it takes a week. You have my word."

Maddon now demanded, harshly, "So what's it to be?"

A buzz of agitated talk came from the cabin, then rifles and guns began to come through the door.

Then a taut voice called, "We're comin' out."

Maddon licked his lips and called from his position on the slope, nearer the cabin now.

"Arms high and easy, boys," he shouted.

Five owlhoots filed out. Maddon's face turned grim to see Pedlar wasn't amongst them.

Cautiously Maddon stepped out to meet the owlhoots, rifle levelled, eyes tawny, fiery and narrow behind the sights.

"Move over here," Maddon ordered. "Where's Pedlar?"

"I've elected to stay, Maddon," Pedlar's voice rasped from the cabin.

As he spoke the gunsels surrendering moved, crouching, hands on heads, as if fearful something was going to happen and they'd be in the middle of it.

Sure enough Pedlar sprang from the open door of the cabin taking Maddon by surprise. But he should have known.

"You ain't takin' me, Maddon!" Pedlar was roaring. "I'm takin' you!"

Maddon could see Pedlar's gun was already out and lining up on him. The damned gunslinger had elected suicide, he thought desperately. Maddon fired instinctively then dropped and rolled and brought the Winchester up again. Hot lead was fanning round him from Pedlar's Colt.

Then he fired a second time and saw Pedlar smashing back into the cabin door, then more shots from the posse savaged the gunslinger's flesh until he fell a mangled corpse, flopping like a banked fish and wallowing in his own blood.

Mean and tired now and cursing his own stupidity for not anticipating Pedlar, Maddon rose from the ground to find blood seeping from a graze across his stomach.

Quickly the posse came out of the trees and Maddon suddenly realised Doc Fredricks was asking him to pull his shirt up so that he could look to his wound.

Even as the sawbones bandaged him, Maddon was asking Marty to take a count. It was found the posse had come through almost unscathed, so good had been the strategy, and Maddon took comfort from that. As Marty pointed out, Maddon himself was the only one hit.

The owlhoots had one man injured. A search found eight bronco corpses in the woods and eight Winchester rifles.

Two missing, thought Maddon. He clamped bitter lips together. Well, you couldn't win them all. Maybe the army would get them . . .

10

THEY left the mountains and rode until late afternoon. They stopped at the Rowel, where they were invited to eat and stay the night.

Mid-afternoon the following day they were tired men filing down Clayton's broad main street, the posse peeling off as they went.

Soon the owlhoots were behind the iron bars of the cells, and Maddon washed thoroughly and shaved in the small back room.

Marty had introduced Shaney Weelon — a tall, gangling man with a long, walrus moustache and narrow grey eyes — as soon as they had arrived. Apparently, he was a sworn-in deputy on a part-time basis who stepped in when wanted.

Now refreshed, Maddon sampled

Sarah Wallace's beef stew, then walked to Wallis Tavener's house to be let in by the sheriff's pretty sister, who welcomed him warmly. Wallis, drawn and pale, was propped up in bed. But he managed a toothy smile before demanding, "Well, say it!"

Maddon told him the story.

When he finished, regret was on Wallis's face. "An' damn it, I missed it," he grumbled.

Maddon grinned. "Why the hell should you have all the fun?"

Tavener returned the grin wryly. "Because I'm the boss!"

"Lay back you ornery longhorn," ordered Maddon. "Can't you enjoy your convalescence?"

Wallis pulled a face. "I'd enjoy a big steak right now, instead of the broth they're fillin' me with." His face grew mournful. "Damn it, I feel like a malingerer in here."

"Doc said you should be dead," Maddon countered. "So be grateful."

Wallis eased back on the pillows,

his face becoming sober. "Yeah," he sighed. "I am as weak as a new-born foal, truth be known."

His narrow blue gaze found Maddon's tawny look. "Frank, you stayin' on?"

"Until you're on your feet, Wallis," he offered. "Then I'll be poundin' new trails."

Tavener nodded as though he had known that would be the answer. "Well, if you ever find a cure for those itchy feet of yours, look me up, eh?"

Maddon nodded, realising he had grown to like this tough little lawman staring up at him from the bed. "You can count on it, Wallis," he said. "Guess I'll be around this way occasionally, visiting with Holly."

★ ★ ★

Snow was powdering the foothills of the Wassala Valley when Maddon urged his bay south.

By then, Wallis was back to full health.

Maddon had come across a few very interesting wanted notices during his time as lawman in Wassala Valley and Wallis had given him some promising information about the habits of a couple of them. And they operated down on the border.

Wrapped against the cold as he moved through the high pass in the southern mountains, he decided he was getting too old for cold night camps and needed the balmy suns of the border on his back . . .

When a man was able, why shouldn't he look for a little comfort?

Maddon smiled grimly to himself at that thought and urged the bay on to the warmer climate ahead, whistling softly.

Other titles in the Linford Western Library:

TOP HAND
Wade Everett

The Broken T was big. But no ranch is big enough to let a man hide from himself.

GUN WOLVES OF LOBO BASIN
Lee Floren

The Feud was a blood debt. When Smoke Talbot found the outlaws who gunned down his folks he aimed to nail their hide to the barn door.

SHOTGUN SHARKEY
Marshall Grover

The westbound coach carrying the indomitable Larry and Stretch headed for a shooting showdown.

FIGHTING RAMROD
Charles N. Heckelmann

Most men would have cut their losses, but Frazer counted the bullets in his guns and said he'd soak the range in blood before he'd give up another inch of what was his.

LONE GUN
Eric Allen

Smoke Blackbird had been away too long. The Lequires had seized the Blackbird farm, forcing the Indians and settlers off, and no one seemed willing to fight! He had to fight alone.

THE THIRD RIDER
Barry Cord

Mel Rawlins wasn't going to let anything stand in his way. His father was murdered, his two brothers gone. Now Mel rode for vengeance.

ARIZONA DRIFTERS
W. C. Tuttle

When drifting Dutton and Lonnie Steelman decide to become partners they find that they have a common enemy in the formidable Thurston brothers.

TOMBSTONE
Matt Braun

Wells Fargo paid Luke Starbuck to outgun the silver-thieving stagecoach gang at Tombstone. Before long Luke can see the only thing bearing fruit in this eldorado will be the gallows tree.

HIGH BORDER RIDERS
Lee Floren

Buckshot McKee and Tortilla Joe cut the trail of a border tough who was running Mexican beef into Texas. They stopped the smuggler in his tracks.

BRETT RANDALL, GAMBLER
E. B. Mann

Larry Day had the choice of running away from the law or of assuming a dead man's place. No matter what he decided he was bound to end up dead.

THE GUNSHARP
William R. Cox

The Eggerleys weren't very smart. They trained their sights on Will Carney and Arizona's biggest blood bath began.

THE DEPUTY OF SAN RIANO
Lawrence A. Keating and
Al. P. Nelson

When a man fell dead from his horse, Ed Grant was spotted riding away from the scene. The deputy sheriff rode out after him and came up against everything from gunfire to dynamite.

FARGO: MASSACRE RIVER
John Benteen

The ambushers up ahead had now blocked the road. Fargo's convoy was a jumble, a perfect target for the insurgents' weapons!

SUNDANCE: DEATH IN THE LAVA
John Benteen

The Modoc's captured the wagon train and its cargo of gold. But now the halfbreed they called Sundance was going after it . . .

HARSH RECKONING
Phil Ketchum

Five years of keeping himself alive in a brutal prison had made Brand tough and careless about who he gunned down . . .

FARGO: PANAMA GOLD
John Benteen

With foreign money behind him, Buckner was going to destroy the Panama Canal before it could be completed. Fargo's job was to stop Buckner.

FARGO: THE SHARPSHOOTERS
John Benteen

The Canfield clan, thirty strong were raising hell in Texas. Fargo was tough enough to hold his own against the whole clan.

PISTOL LAW
Paul Evan Lehman

Lance Jones came back to Mustang for just one thing — revenge! Revenge on the people who had him thrown in jail.

HELL RIDERS
Steve Mensing

Wade Walker's kid brother, Duane, was locked up in the Silver City jail facing a rope at dawn. Wade was a ruthless outlaw, but he was smart, and he had vowed to have his brother out of jail before morning!

DESERT OF THE DAMNED
Nelson Nye

The law was after him for the murder of a marshal — a murder he didn't commit. Breen was after him for revenge — and Breen wouldn't stop at anything . . . blackmail, a frameup . . . or murder.

DAY OF THE COMANCHEROS
Steven C. Lawrence

Their very name struck terror into men's hearts — the Comancheros, a savage army of cutthroats who swept across Texas, leaving behind a bloodstained trail of robbery and murder.

SUNDANCE: SILENT ENEMY
John Benteen

A lone crazed Cheyenne was on a personal war path. They needed to pit one man against one crazed Indian. That man was Sundance.

LASSITER
Jack Slade

Lassiter wasn't the kind of man to listen to reason. Cross him once and he'll hold a grudge for years to come — if he let you live that long.

LAST STAGE TO GOMORRAH
Barry Cord

Jeff Carter, tough ex-riverboat gambler, now had himself a horse ranch that kept him free from gunfights and card games. Until Sturvesant of Wells Fargo showed up.

McALLISTER ON THE COMANCHE CROSSING
Matt Chisholm

The Comanche, McAllister owes them a life — and the trail is soaked with the blood of the men who had tried to outrun them before.

QUICK-TRIGGER COUNTRY
Clem Colt

Turkey Red hooked up with Curly Bill Graham's outlaw crew. But wholesale murder was out of Turk's line, so when range war flared he bucked the whole border gang alone . . .

CAMPAIGNING
Jim Miller

Ambushed on the Santa Fe trail, Sean Callahan is saved by two Indian strangers. But there'll be more lead and arrows flying before the band join Kit Carson against the Comanches.

GUNSLINGER'S RANGE
Jackson Cole

Three escaped convicts are out for revenge. They won't rest until they put a bullet through the head of the dirty snake who locked them behind bars.

RUSTLER'S TRAIL
Lee Floren

Jim Carlin knew he would have to stand up and fight because he had staked his claim right in the middle of Big Ike Outland's best grass.

THE TRUTH ABOUT SNAKE RIDGE
Marshall Grover

The troubleshooters came to San Cristobal to help the needy. For Larry and Stretch the turmoil began with a brawl and then an ambush.

WOLF DOG RANGE
Lee Floren

Will Ardery would stop at nothing, unless something stopped him first — like a bullet from Pete Manly's gun.

DEVIL'S DINERO
Marshall Grover

Plagued by remorse, a rich old reprobate hired the Texas Troubleshooters to deliver a fortune in greenbacks to each of his victims.

GUNS OF FURY
Ernest Haycox

Dane Starr, alias Dan Smith, wanted to close the door on his past and hang up his guns, but people wouldn't let him.